Nurtured Blood

Nurtured Blood

Priscila K.

To my dad, Paulus Guani K.

Please control your diet

Love you

1

⌇

Inner Speech

A diminutive crystal vessel reflecting what other people see when they look at me - I'm spinning it right now with the majority of my fingers, gracefully, but in a peculiar way like my head is the one spinning inside. Maybe my head is the one that's moving, I don't know.

But there's something else interesting about this pellucid thing. There, I can see myself turn delicate orange. They smell briny, sweet, and fishy. A tempting piece of glass, I'd say; the interior is filled with a slice of swirled smoked trout garnished with a little bit of dill and rosemary. It explains the yummy smell ready for my bite.

But enough now about food.

I'm talking to myself in my head again. Sigh. I always do, especially whenever I'm surrounded by these boring intellectual chatters - *soigné* with their judging eyes, always talk about what's new in the economy. No wonder I never really fit in here. Whenever they bore me, I always let myself get distracted, just like with this fine piquant canapé.

To tell you the truth, they're not always boring. I quite enjoy their company whenever they ask me about things that don't matter. "Do you enjoy your study?" No. "How is your work?" Awful. "When are you going to quit?" Actually, already did. Especially whenever they don't ask any further questions to my terse answer like they're never interested from the beginning, I love it. You could say I enjoy more of this - wondering what they think when they look at me.

I add a smile in between occasionally, and nod from time to time. It's quite whimsical that they think my smile means I'm naturally trying my best to listen to what they're talking about and just eventually not getting the conversation, when really, I'm just not listening at all. But they're probably right too. I really don't get it sometimes. Don't know or don't care; honestly, I don't even know anymore.

Actually, they're very wonderful people, interestingly. Uncle Gershom with his fat belly and glossy hair on my left, Mrs. Oriel in the middle with her distracting big red jewel on her neck, and Sir Halihan looking like a misunderstood gangster in a super fancy suit. Actually, Sir Halihan is more like a big scary penguin to me. Well, that's fun to imagine. I'd be a doozie drowsy koala,

Uncle Gershom a teddy bear came to life, so that would make Mrs. Oriel... a white peafowl.

But seriously, this conversation at the moment about some new government policy raising interest rates and how to make more money out of it is just plain boring. Even worse when they ask my opinion about it. Easier to shrug my shoulders so I don't have to think. No pressure's best. I could probably think of something but I'd definitely say the wrong thing anyway, so why do I even bother? I mean, the right answer keeps slipping out of my mind, every time, even when I've learned about it. That kind of knowledge is like a dry glue to me, it just never sticks. And my brain is like a monolith when it's uninterested, but it's probably because I'm just not smart enough.

Ugh, honestly, 'what's for dinner' seems more interesting to be discussed. Actually, if they'd rather talk about the food... Would they?

Who am I kidding? They wouldn't.

You know what? Nevermind, I'll just keep quiet.

I've just got to escape.

Succeedingly with an enormous amount of effort to get out of the conversation politely, I'm able to get to the kitchen uninvitedly to speak with one of the chefs; I just couldn't take it anymore. The scent in this room feels so different to me. It still smells the same fishy good, even stronger than before; but I also smell peace, and this is exactly what my mind needs.

Dear friendly, talented, but slightly arrogant Monsieur Scerri with his blonde hair and twisted moustache is succinctly communicating the steps to me about how the little dish of joy was brought out into the world. He's doing so while getting the rest of these little canapés out to the guests. He's clearly good at juggling between working with his hands and talking with his mouth. I find it funny sometimes to see his yellow moustache moving along with his maroon lips. His fingers look shiny slippery from the oily condiment but it seems to support his speed rather than slowing him down.

"So I soaked just enough gelatine leaves in cold water to be drained and squeezed *all the way* - this is very important. Then, I added them to the stock and stirred until they're completely dissolved. After that, I sprayed just enough oil inside the glass mould, broke the smoked trout *elegantly* with my fingers, and divided the trout between the moulds, just so I could fill each with the jellied stock in the middle. I refrigerated them for about six hours and *voilà*! Beautiful like a painting, yes?"

Very interesting.

It got me thinking though. I'd have probably been better off taking a painting or culinary major than some mainstream business degree in a great university that I took, which seems to have limited my option from a blow to the ego once to instead leave everything behind.

Maybe do some other things, like being a street artist for a change in this family; if only I have the courage and the talent. Free of pressure, full of passion, constantly standing on the temptation border between maximum creativity with no boundary and getting into jail for trespassing. Besides, I'm never really fond of remembering instructions, moreover following them.

Or maybe a career like Monsieur Scerri's; he seems pretty content with his work. I've already got a bunch of tips from him anyway and it's probably not too late for me to start. And I do love eating, too much, that I sometimes wonder if I really do. But then again, I'm pretty sure I'd get fired within two hours of probation for eating too much customers' food looking too delicious, out of the obvious kitchen stress with no cooking contribution from myself.

I'm not even kidding. I'm pretty sure this would happen. It's the worst possible outcome when the heart is more to take than to serve. You could also say, I'm prone to be against following orders most of the time. I just like to do my own thing. So everywhere I go, I feel like I'm already bound for disruption and destruction.

It's in my nature. I like my freedom fully intact no matter the consequences. So in that case, I'd really rather eat them in front of the boss chef, get fired, then laugh about it in my sleep.

In some such way, that really happened.

2

~

The Accident

"So, Daedalia..."

Daedalia - that's my name. Some people say it's a beautiful name, that it's unique, but I don't like it one bit. It just verifies the confusion in me.

"What are your plans now, dear?"

Oh right, someone's talking to me.

Her French accent accompanied by the movement of wrinkles around her bright red lips startles me just a bit, and I don't even think she can actually speak French. It also confuses me sometimes why I still need to call her *Madame*. It matches her appearance though. Tall and skinny, teal green evening wear, high bun tied with golden ribbon matching her grey-painted-black hair - looking elegant forty in her sixties. Her body reflects that of a crowded gemstone runway, jewels all over. And I bet she's still doing hot yoga.

Madame Hilda sounds concerned and really wants to know what I'm going to do, to gossip to the rest I'm sure. She looks and sounds like she has that kind of mouth every time she speaks.

This is after I quit my job on behalf of my impulsivity and damaged curiosity not too long ago. Formidable company, owned by a big private company owned by a bigger private company owned by another bigger private company.

Imagine hundreds of blurry faces as your background when you work, thousands more somewhere else you don't even know where. No one really notices you either, because you're also one of the blurry ones. In fact, if you show up unannounced behind their back, they might think you're a *ghost*.

You can even do the work as you please, if you act stupid. You're not even aware of the politics already going on about speed climbing the corporate ladder, and you don't really have to be, because everyone's for themselves anyway. It's like making yourself the lost sheep and you don't even care because you actually like being lost, or being the sheep. You even think you taste good as supper for the wolves; it's much easier to lie down on the plate and sleep. It's too stressful to become one of the wolves anyway, you actually have to work for it, often at midnight when everyone else is already fast asleep.

Technically, you'll just be buying your time before you get skipped or sacked.

Perfect if you don't want the chance of ruining your family

business by running it. You tend to be more careless when it's not something you own, being careless requires less or no paying attention at all, and acting in ignorance means you're already on the loose because you have no more sense of responsibility left in you. You become like the wind; either you blow into the breeze or you blow to ruin, it's entirely up to you.

It's a great job, I won't deny it. Too good to be true for someone like me, except that I'm not that kind who values being employed by someone else other than myself. So for anyone who really knew me, they could already tell that I was already deciding on quitting the second I started. All I had to do was to convince myself that I loved the job and just like that, I was losing my reason. So that *accident*, that really was to be expected.

"Well, I'm still on this journey..."

Ahem, bullpoop alert.

"Finding my true *passion*..."

Blah blah blah.

"What I really want to do in life is changing the world..."

Wait, what world is it again that I'm trying to change?

"I haven't really got a clue..."

Finally, I get some honesty out.

"I guess in the meantime that is the plan. I'm still discovering the field."

There you go. And I even finish my reply with a bit of a smile, an awkward kind.

Discovering the field. Sigh. More like discovering myself.

But to tell you the truth, I've never been happier - you know, being unemployed and poor. Good thing I resigned; though theoretically, I got fired. Well, I screamed "I quit" seconds before I got fired, so technically I wasn't fired, right? All I did was crash my client's excavator into the empty portable office so horribly *by mistake* that everything collapsed, but my ex-colleagues still think I did it on purpose.

Still a complete mystery to me if I really did, to be honest. All I remember, my mind went blank as it happened. I sneaked in of course, and the thought of really crashing it for the adrenaline had really crossed my mind many times before. Was I really that curious that I'd risk my life just to know how it'd be? Was I really that bored that my mind craved for some drama in my life? Or was it my surrounding for having nothing interesting to talk about that I thought I'd give them one? Don't get me wrong; I totally get it, that it wasn't anyone's fault but me.

But I took it as they didn't value my curiosity. Although, there's a bit of self-destruction and self-sabotage too there; at times I notice, and maybe they all do too. I really thought I was never going to have another chance to ride (or crash) it when I was about to quit anyway. I mean, if I needed some technicality to make myself feel better that at least my short time there was not a waste, this would be it, the perfect ending.

Who am I kidding? I deserved it, the total blame. I mean, I almost got the client and the boss killed from a heart attack, just because I was bored. That's it, I think that's the real answer - I was just bored.

"Ah, *passion*. Yes, of course, dear. You'll find it, someday. Don't worry, dear."

She seems happy with my concealed answer of life boredom,

lost ambition, and drained excitement. But wait, is that a bit of a frown I'm seeing there?

"As a matter of fact, we don't actually need it, dear. It's just *interim decorum* for us women to feel important. Start thinking about marriage, dear; you know, with the kind of my late husb... your cousins are married to. Expand the family fortune. Give back to your family with an heir or two. After all, *passion* is a dangerous word, dear. No harm intended, dear. Just speaking the truth. 'They' do expire."

Excuse me?

And apparently now she speaks pure Latin.

Not to mention there's just really too many of the word 'dear' when she speaks, that actually annoys me more than the value of her words already does.

I should've probably expected the response. But my family's money is not my money, especially if I don't go their way - told you I was poor. So of course they expect the women to settle down quickly and have babies with business emperors if they want to make themselves most useful. Ugh, boring! My only solution is to make it on my own and prove them wrong. The only problem is, I haven't got a clue how. I mean, this idiot doesn't even know what she is or where she is in life right now. She's completely useless.

It's already a horrible feeling for me not to know what I'm actually really good at, providing I'm actually good at something. It's additionally awful when I don't even know what I actually really want to do in this life; up to this point, I only know the things that I don't want to do, and so far that's about everything

I needed to do. Much more annoying when I constantly have no idea why I'm still doing all these things I'm doing.

Finding one's true self is not easy, even when they think I already have everything I need, and that just makes me complain about the things I already have. Maybe I should just stop aiming to indulge in life and start to search for abstract wisdom instead; you know, like a real purpose. Will that make me stop complaining? There's nothing more to lose in my life anyway. I've really got nothing left; though I think, I've still got a little bit of backup if I just surrender. But that just makes me sound complacent like some people here that I don't really like.

Sigh. All of us in this neighbourhood, really. Our ancestors have got it all covered, they say. And if we ever get lost, we think we will always have that backup prepared by the dead before us just by turning around, going back home - as simple as that. Lady, I don't even know where the list of the assets is, but I know there isn't going to be that much left for us. Especially if we're keeping Monsieur Scerri alike on the weekly payroll. Should probably tune down on that first-class travelling and caviar dining once in a while too, caviar doesn't even taste that good. None of us is actually that keen on earning either; other than spending money, showing off to one another, and having no interest and sense of responsibility in taking care of what our ancestors had built. And it's... a lot to adjust. I guess there really is such thing as being tired of proving your worth in dollar terms.

I've changed a lot since my travel days, away from this place.

But isn't that mere shiny piece of academic paper should have been enough to prove that I did give their lacklustre way a try? That I now have my right to move on with my life my own way without their judging eyes? Whichever way that is. Considering that was actually my only goal with all of this; basically something to validate, some self-worthy recognition away from my diffidence, until I crashed that excavator of course. That completely ruined my image and there's no way my reputation is turning back from there.

But didn't I already deserve to live my life my own way without judgement and not to fulfil some sort of common expectations from society? What if I just don't want to marry? What if I just don't want to settle down here? Maybe I just want to live in all of these places instead; Dubrovnik, Okinawa, or maybe Timbuktu. Anywhere but *here*.

I'll start my controversial journey with the common route, from the west of 'peninsula of the peninsulas'. Incipiently a redo, but this time with a different mindset to adhere to. I'm still a bit pissed off that I was too young when I first went, like it was just some sort of a race between foes and friends of whose bucket list was ticked the earliest, and taking photos for the proud trophy was the priority - I don't even look good in any of them. And because of all that stupid list, I don't even remember having a good time there; the trip was just tiring. The worst part is, I don't even feel I learned anything from it. Fifteen countries and I still know nothing.

But I did enjoy the view of Paris, and I don't mean that

naked couple I saw up the River Seine. Cuckoo clocks fascinate me more since my last visit to Triberg; I secretly want to learn how to make one now. I love how I ate so much in Sicily but never gained weight. Cried of wonders in Geneva though I cried of pain breaking my younger back worse than an old lady did in Titlis, just because I was trying to show off to her; how stupid. My younger mind was just really stupid.

Still so many places to visit. Maybe I just want to be a nomad until the day I die. Like doing bingo but with my life. I know this conversation got my father riled up before. Daddy said free spirit was never a good trait to have in a woman. Unfortunately, that's the only trait I've ascertained of me. Explains why I almost got expelled from boarding school, and there were even no boys to influence me.

But seriously, what is the point of living anyway when a portion of your life is more for the things you hate than the things you love?

My face is balloon red from cogitating and I think I can burst any moment now. She's expecting an answer and I know she means *kinda* well, but I don't think she will appreciate a counterblast. This society - her eyes threaten me menacingly - judging my every action, every reaction, every second. Ticking time bomb - she rapidly stomps her right hindfoot - demanding her opinion to be my immediate resolution to my lost sense of direction that she will call realisation.

I'm still quiet, consciously swallowing my saliva repetitively like my gland is an emerging wellspring, and she's still relentlessly waiting for a response.

I need a fake answer. Hurry, brain!

...

Nothing

...

Nope, still got nothing.

...

Sigh. I've got nothing.

No choice. I guess this time, I'll have to say what's really on my mind.

Ding-a-ling ding-a-ling ding-a-ling.

My luck, we've got a distraction.

3

~

Silent Observation

The dinner bell that sounds like a very loud tintinnabulation on a Sunday morning manages to stop my train of thoughts and my obligation to respond. Everyone is now heading to the enormously long dinner table awaiting all the oddly consistent twelve people. The spaces between us are just insane, no table should be this long. I hope they are all aware that none of us is actually royalty. This kind of dinner setup for any common event is extremely unnecessary.

What has brought us together so regularly? For most of us, it's the same neighbourhood we all live in, with only walking distance afar if we don't even bother to drive. We can choose to be chauffeured, pampered even within such a short reach, but I still favour the walk. It helps me clear my tangled thoughts. Usually the longer the better. My calves have been trained so vigorously from walking for so many hours, mostly to find a way back home because I keep getting distracted by the other road at intersections - just like my thoughts.

"There you are! Where have you been?"

My mom sounds worried, but her social-butterfly element must have stopped her from coming to find me ages of hours ago.

She was in the centre of the living room the whole time where everyone else predominantly was; along with Aunt Petunia 'the host', who has somehow been looking rather pale and weak these past few weeks. Consistently on every occasion too, she still forces herself to look her prettiest like she isn't in any pain even though she obviously is, something even her heavy makeup cannot hide. Sometimes I wonder if it's all on purpose, like a super dangerous diet. I mean, she already looked like a walking skeleton before, but now even her bones look almost invisible. It's like she could almost disappear within sight any time soon.

"I've been near the kitchen, Mom."

From the look of her face, she doesn't seem to remember where it is. Besides, this is a pretty big mansion. It has been in the possession of my uncle, Gershom Pavirsia, and his wife, Petunia Eastaughffe, for many years now.

Similar to my mom, Eleanor, Aunt Petunia doesn't take her husband's last name. My mom, whose surname is Abernathy, is so proud of her surname for some reason, she had hers added to both her two children's. Should have been for no reason, so I don't have to bear this stupidly-long surname. Aunt Petunia, however, has the ultimate simple reason not to - she just doesn't want to. Too lazy dealing with those boring documents, she must be.

My mom and Aunt Petunia; they both always seem (or act) very close in person every time they meet, but the truth is, their relationship is only as far as a chance occurrence to meet at family events. In consequence, I'm never as close to my cousin, Idonia Pavirsia.

Idonia is very quiet, always. I've never in my life ever seen the thirteen year-old initiate a conversation with anyone. She also only smiles if people smile at her first, only then she will move her lips. For someone her age, she behaves very maturely, poise and sumptuous, probably because of her parents' heavy influence on her; but perhaps she's just being weary of the people here, I can relate with that. I could see her being tired of the same boring conversations, then her presence being missing, until that sound of the dinner bell ringing brought all of us together and made us look small in this insanely gigantic dining room. This dining room is indeed extensively palatial. This is probably the most spacious room here, not to mention glorious, being located just on the corner of this great mansion. You know how they say corner rooms are always the biggest.

One way or another, Idonia and I, we both seem pretty similar, except that I never see her near the kitchen. Her hiding spot must be different to mine; not what currently is, not even the previous one. I did change my hiding spot; it was getting too predictable. Regardless, we could probably be really good friends if our age is not twelve years apart, or if we have the same hiding spot.

Idonia is sitting right in front of me while looking down with her fingers twirling the little golden hourglass pendant around her neck when all of a sudden, her eyes see straight to mine. After about two seconds, I smile at the little girl. As I expect, she smiles back at me. Her smile looks so innocent that I even feel bad to stop my smiling before she does.

It quickly stops nonetheless, as soon as the waiters bring in the main course for the night, distracting the both of us. Twelve aromatic plates plus twelve empty wine glasses are added into the celebration. No appetisers because the host doesn't eat much, more like doesn't eat at all. But she's the host; so long there's still food on the table for us, I don't have any reason to complain.

Chicken Ballotine.

I've already known the name even before the server speaks of it.

The dish in front of me looks like a big fat white sausage on a golden pillow of sweet potato puree. Seems a bit naked in my opinion, not enough of a blanket of sauce to cover its body. It's still very pretty though, with colourful edible flowers and fresh vegetables covering almost half of the plate like a wild garden. I'm slicing through the chicken and can now see the brown-coloured minced meats inside. I'm tasting it and...

Wow, I did not expect this at all! These crunchy bits. There's also bacon inside, quite lots of it, along with minced pork and chicken cooked through and stirred with what feels to me are thyme and rosemary. Wonderful. And the saltiness from the bacon doesn't even overpower the rest of the dish as I thought it would.

"I suppose the wine is coming very soon?"

Doctor Godric has just distracted our mind from the delectable main course we're all still enjoying.

Now that I think of him, I've never talked to him that much about anything, although I seem to always see him around. I don't even think he lives around the block. Actually, why is he always here?

Doctor Godric touches his spectacles a lot. I notice that his nose is a bit crooked so that pair of glasses look like they're sitting perfectly on his face. He also always seems so reserved. Even my super talkative mom has not been able to penetrate his mind to speak more to her than he feels necessary to; and as she grows tired of it, she just stops trying eventually. He's still a total mystery to me in so many ways, despite what feels like the thousandth time that we've met.

I can see some eyes are revolving quite strangely at him now. Maybe because he speaks up about the wine? I mean, an incredibly quiet man such as him has the audacity to raise his voice in front of everybody to remind us about the empty glass of wine. I perceive he always does this kind of thing when he looks nervous the most. That could explain that weird glass-waving gesture I saw at a glance earlier. Possibly, he just loves wine that much? If yes, that's one more thing I can add to my list of him - a quiet doctor with a dark vibe that seems to really love his wine.

"Well, what kind of *fiesta* forgets about pouring wine into these empty glasses? Maybe someone needs to get sacked first before everyone's able to do their job properly. And Petunia, it's going to be one of those *exorbitant* wines from Barossa, yes?"

Miss Decima Somerset, one of Aunt Petunia's socialite and younger friends.

She seems unhappy with the unprofessionalism she thinks the waiters inhabit; though I don't think it's their fault by how they've been serving us. With approximately twenty years of gap between their age, I sometimes wonder how it all started - their friendship.

I don't even think I like Miss Decima that much, that whole attitude of hers; actually, I never do. But every time I wish I won't be turning into someone like her, I think I slowly am. The classic, turning into someone you hate. I mean, the signs are already there. She's making herself unemployed and using her family's money to "explore herself", just because she thinks working is stopping her from "finding her true destiny"; she really did say those exact same words. She doesn't even bother helping the family business because she thinks she will ruin it anyway; she doesn't like the sense of responsibility it brings. She also "quit" her job, she did mention; but instead of crashing something, I heard she *stabbed* someone. Like literally, with a knife. It might not be true though, as some people here already think I crashed that excavator to kill someone for no reason, like I was some sort of psycho. I did kill, but it was something not someone - my reputation. They should've got that part of the fact right at least.

But there just seems to be a background story resulting in her mysterious uncivil behaviour. Sometimes, somehow, I don't even think she means the worst in whatever comes out of her mouth; but one thing that I really really really hate about what's coming out of her mouth is how she always intentionally smokes her fancy cigar and blows it in front of her surroundings' faces. Regardless, to the displeasure of poor us near her at her utmost delight. Even now, while we're eating. For goodness' sake, Lady Rude. She's lucky she's pretty, scary, and always holds the cigar like a knife as if she can toss it anytime and burn the skin of anyone that pisses her off.

"Petunia, you seem to be very quiet these days. What's wrong with you, honey? Why aren't you even looking excited on your birthday?"

Mrs. Oriel, who seems to be the closest to Aunt Petunia, voices out her concern.

Compared to Miss Decima, Mrs. Oriel is probably the better influence on Aunt Petunia. She seems very kind and caring towards her. Her eyebrows are forming a rainbow the whole time she's talking to Aunt Petunia, her expression really shows she's deeply worried about her. That somehow makes me think that she's genuinely disturbed by Aunt Petunia's sudden change of behaviour.

She's right though.

The Aunt Petunia that I knew would immediately bang the table, stand up angrily, barge into the pantry, and start firing people. Not to mention it's her birthday today. Otherwise, why else the twelve of us, who actually have nothing better to do anyway, have gathered here on this beautiful sundown hour in her house with our best cocktail dress. With her usually being the competitive social butterfly to my mother, it's almost un-believable to see her so quiet and letting my mom fly solo with both her hyperactive wings this evening. So I also suspect some-thing's wrong.

The Aunt Petunia that I'm looking at right now is just responding with a forced smile with her right hand still glued on her forehead. Rather than looking excited, she just seems woozy and sleepy, wishing the dinner to be over soon so she can quickly get on her bed and rest.

Uncle Gershom, looking a bit embarrassed, is about to stand up until he's stopped by Aunt Petunia's ahem and waving right hand. Her face shows a bit of confusion, just like Uncle's; but out of the blue, she still gently offers herself to get up and sort things out peacefully, unlike that diva attitude she often showed in the past.

"I'll go, dear. Besides, I think I need to go to the powder room. Still feeling a bit dizzy, for days, weeks now, mind you."

Uncle Gershom who's sitting far away across from her seems to be relieved and worried at the same time; but as obedient as he has always been to her, he speaks no word to confirm the agreement.

So off she goes.

4

Boring Realm

It took almost ten minutes for Aunt Petunia to show up again, along with two servers on both sides. The one standing on her left is Rayner and the other one is Lothar. They're the same ones that distributed the main course and empty wine glasses previously.

They're both bringing two bottles of red, one each. Lothar is taking the side by the window to the door on my left if I look to my right, while Rayner is in charge of the rest. I'm pretty sure it has always been the same as that must be how they're taught by Mr. Catullus - the head butler whose name seems to be derived from a famous poet's; as I habitually sit on the right side of the table with both of my parents, it has always been Rayner who serves us too. It's almost strange to me how it feels like every one of us knows 'our place' around this table, but it feels even stranger to think about wherelese we would sit.

I think if Rayner pursues a career as an actor, he can really make it. He's really tall and good looking, except maybe his thick eyebrows need a bit of a trim. But sometimes I wonder if he's actually a robot. He doesn't talk like one, but he acts like it in some ways. Like that lovely smile of his, always starts with exactly two seconds without teeth, then three seconds with, and ends with a bit of sniffing then one ahem. His eyes are also always closed every one and a half second. I really did count. Either I was that bored or accidentally in love.

Anyway, Aunt Petunia looks better though. With a glimpse of water drops on her face, it appears that she has just visited the restroom.

"Golly! The wine was displaced from its usual spot. The most expensive one, mind you. And yes! It's of the oldest vine from that chateau in Tanunda. As you know, I never settle for less," she finally shows one of her usual selves, and I mean that kind - those who don't really know anything about wine so they always choose the most expensive one.

No further questions are asked as the wine is poured in each of every glass. Doctor Godric must be so happy, though he doesn't really look like he is. As the wine drama officially ends after the last poured glass, Uncle Gershom eventually stands to say the words he has obviously memorised to set the mood in the room back to its celebration origin.

"Ahem ahem. A toast to the wonderful wife of mine, Petunia, who never wishes to grow old but never seems to look a year older even on her *fiftieth* birthday, and cheers for another fifty to come. Happy birthday, my love!"

What a bad move, in my opinion. I can't believe after all these years, he really said that - that Aunt Petunia is now officially fifty years old. I don't think Uncle was doing it on purpose, but he was just rubbing it in. Knowing how we're all aware that Aunt Petunia hates to be reminded of her real age, her face shows an involuntary grin to the toast like she's ready to kill uncle later before bed time. But everyone is kindly forcing a smile so he'll think that dying in Aunt Petunia's hand will all be worth it.

Everyone is then standing up and singing the happy birthday song commonly sung here in the neighbourhood, which I notice isn't regularly sung or even known elsewhere.

"Happy Birthday, we are all singing to you
The melody is tuned full and bright, just for you
The sky is joining us, whether it is dark or blue
Long live to you!
Too, wish all of your dreams come true
Happy Birthday, we will sing again to you
Next year!"

The woman with plump chubby cheeks does it again with her voice, every time, no matter how tense the aura in the room is.

Mrs. Lesley, who lives right next to my parents' residence, seems to really fancy her singing skill, considering her voice is the loudest from the beginning to end. Everyone is clapping and I think it's solely to give thanks to the former opera singer's sonorous voice for covering most of our hasty and questioning carolling expertise. And she's just doing it gladly; I know she adores the praise. Her proud smile can't be more obvious than that, silently screaming for more.

Everyone's straight drinking the wine as soon as the last lyric hits the roof. Afterward, they're all picking up where their conversation left off while I'm just thinking about what the dessert will be. I can hear some people saying how full they already are. If my true manner is excused in this universe, I can probably have some more of theirs. One portion is usually not that much when Aunt Petunia is hosting.

As I'm quickly getting bored again of the current conversation on the table, I'm looking to my right to see what's going on with the sky just because the birthday song mentions it; I'm giving myself a reason to space out as always. It mostly works, transporting to a whole different world in my mind by looking the other way, away from all of these boring conversations where even a single eye contact can drag me in that quickly; it will be harder to pull myself out this time.

Wait, Aunt Petunia?
What's wrong with her?

Aunt Petunia's breath seems to deteriorate and she looks as pale as a trapped white mouse.

"Aunt Petunia, are you okay?"

I speak up loudly by instinct so everyone notices.

Between me and Idonia - we're sitting closest to her - I seem to be the quickest to embrace her body-in-pain, while the little red-haired is standing like a statue and looking extremely worried.

In response, Aunt Petunia presses her left hand to her chest then neck with her ongoing shallow breathing. Her right hand pushes hard on the table later following her left to the throat as the choking strives. In an instant too, everyone's screaming Doctor Godric's name. He already runs to Aunt Petunia's chair as soon as his eyes set straight to her suffering, just like Uncle Gershom and everybody else sitting further from her.

With Doctor Godric and the others just a few inches away from her, she falls to my arms which I immediately drop towards the floor to catch her, and she ... stops breathing?

I move her head onto Doctor Godric's thighs and her legs onto Uncle Gershom's. I have no idea what else I can do to help her. He's the doctor, I'm not. Everything is happening so fast that I rapidly feel futile for not being able to do more than I can. Can he save her? Does Aunt Petunia still have a chance?

"She's ... gone."
Doctor Godric's face turns more white in colour; he's still speaking up, horrified.

Uncle Gershom and Idonia are now circling around her lifeless body that is now getting cold; the closest, still frozen.

What's going on? Is it a heart attack? She was still alive just a couple of minutes ago, and now she's... dead?

I still can't believe it. Everything's happening so fast and none of us has even had the chance to call the ambulance yet. My mind is still processing to keep up with the death event before me.

Everyone's starting to cry and scream. Simultaneously, they're asking Doctor Godric what has just happened, then they keep on repeating the question.

"I... can't say for sure, until I get her to autopsy."

"Certainly not!" Uncle Gershom suddenly screams. "Call the ambulance and bring her back to life!"

He continues his longing and I can feel his pain as he's voicing it. I'm still in complete silence until I see what I'm seeing, Miss Decima picking up her glass of wine from the table while her hands are still greatly trembling.

"STOP! EVERYONE, DON'T TOUCH ANYTHING!"

That is me, screaming; without my own head even having enough time to process whether it's the right thing to say, let alone screaming it. I don't even know what's going on and why Aunt Petunia suddenly drops dead, but I have a strong feeling that there's something more to this; my surmise, strongly believing this somehow, and that's why I did it.

I can see that everyone's looking at me now, the way when Doctor Godric shouted about the wine. The Daedalia Pavirsia-Abernathy, who famously never speaks up about anything, has just screamed to everyone in the room as if a different soul has forcingly entered her body.

I realise now, as I'm calmly calling the ambulance and the police without being instructed to do so, even when everyone's still acting like a statue; it must be those crime fiction novels I can't stop reading, then brought up to my dream, that my instinct is getting on top of me to stop everyone from touching anything in the room regardless. Except this time, it's not a fiction and I'm not in the book; I'm in the story that's really happening in real life.

Am I finally living my dream in this boring realm called reality?

Is this a nightmare or something else?

"They're on their way shortly," I proceed on speaking beneath the silence.

5

∽

My Old Hiding Spot

"Young lady, you need to wait in the next room, just like the others!"

The police officer speaks, screams, only right at me - one of the two witnesses who's still in this room.

Doctor Godric is next to me, still kneeling next to Aunt Petunia's body. He's looking quite unfocused and excessively sweating somehow, like he's never seen a dead body before. Wouldn't he have seen at least one already during his study? I thought he was one of those surgeons. He's looking a bit embarrassing compared to that rustic and bald old man with white short beard and big glasses next to him. He's a doctor too, one of those crime scene experts. His face looks more like he's calmly reading and flipping through a newspaper instead of a dead body. That old man is acting more like a real doctor. But if

I'm being nice, maybe because Aunt Petunia isn't just another stranger to Doctor Godric.

I always thought that I would be the type to run away as soon as I saw an actual dead body right in front of me, especially someone familiar. I seem to have underrated my courage somehow, because here I am, still looking at my aunt's dead body. I repeat, my aunt's dead body. Also, still ignoring the furious police officer standing behind me who wishes to get me out of the room immediately. The thought of his owl-looking eyes at hand behind my back really annoys me. Even I look way calmer than Doctor Godric, but he's the one that gets to stay.

I roll my eyes without that police officer knowing, just to physically point out my frustration. My ill judgement tells me I should move even closer to the corpse just to annoy him back.

Garlic?

Hang on, there's a bit of garlic smell from Aunt Petunia's mouth.

I'm moving my nose even closer to her pale dead face when suddenly that police officer grabs me by the shoulder to the back and urges me to leave immediately. He clearly implies he's had enough of me.

Fine!

I walk away slowly from the body. Doctor Godric follows me out of the door shortly after. My guess is, that police officer actually wanted both of us to leave but didn't dare to do the same to Doctor Godric. I have to admit, that was very smart of him, using me as bait. Or, could be that he was scared he'd kill Doctor Godric for the doctor's been looking dying ever since; one single touch might jump start that dead face of him and bring him to an actual death.

But about that garlic.

I never think that I'm a genius; I don't think I ever once demonstrated that photogenic-memory skill geniuses always seem to have, at least when I'm awake - I still think I'm an idiot. But I do clearly remember one thing. I noticed there was never any garlic in any of the dishes here, ever. But can I trust my memory this time, that my instinct is somehow not distorted by my curiosity?

"Honey, what is happening with you? Why are you suddenly behaving like this?"

My dad approaches me as soon as I enter the set waiting room, worried obviously.

"Is this going to be like that excavator drama again? God, not again!" My mom jumps in.

"I was just curious. I'm sorry, not going to do it again," I reply to avoid further peculiarity I already exhibit to the rest of the room.

Not that I meant it. Definitely positive that I'm going to do it again. No regret.

I've witnessed the murder this close with my own eyes. I've

become an eyewitness just like the others around me with the same statutory eyes, but I don't think what I'm feeling right now is the same as theirs. Seeing a scene like this in real life, instead of a book or a television, it feels completely different. It still feels like I'm really inside the story, with a real unprecedented tail of events before me. I just want to keep on flipping the pages, keep on watching, and find out about the ending as it goes.

I'm now sitting with my right leg going up and down like I'm forgetting my manners. The officers are keeping us on a watch and making sure we're not talking to each other, so naturally I'm brainstorming in my head everything that I want to do that I know is obviously going to get the officers and investigators' blood pressure rising.

One vacuous idea pops up in my head. It's so stupid, but I have to do it very quickly before I miss the chance if I want to give it a try. I have to do that one-two-three thing you do when you hesitate.

Pretending to go to the restroom, I wish to speak to one of the officers - the one's in charge.

"I will ask everyone questions in the reading room one by one, so I'd suggest for your curious mind to go back to the living room where the others are," Detective Jevon talks to me politely, but the tone is as if he has already heard the rebel side of me; that police officer must have ratted me out.

Thinking about Detective Jevon's face, I want to give him an input that his sharp jawline can really benefit from trimming his beard once in a while; but based on his odour and worn-out leather jacket, I don't think he's going to care anyway. There's even a leftover lettuce on his thick left eyebrow, how did it even get up there? Most importantly, still about the lettuce, how can it even be stuck there for so long? Was there any glue in the sauce? I hope for his sake that he won't be falling in love with Miss Decima. The world might have to turn upside down first before there was even a slight possibility that she would consider him.

"Can I be the first one?" I reply; he seems startled with my response.

Little does he know the rascal idea I've had in mind.

Actually, stupid is more what it is, as to what I am. But even when you do stupid things, because you're stupid, that can sometimes get you even further than those smart ones. Well, because they'll think it's stupid and won't do it. And if you succeed, they'll call that stupid act as being courageous and cleverly calculative instead of being foolish and incredibly lucky, calling it a smart move; suddenly, you're not so stupid anymore. I'm betting on this right now. This, or both my curiosity and impulsivity already get the better judgement in me.

In a hurry, I'm running to the reading room wishing that it'll still be empty. Yes, it still is! And it's not even locked. So I'm going to the bookshelves I'm already very familiar with, more than the owners, more than the maids, down to the elusive dust spots. This room used to be my hiding spot before it got too obvious that it was.

With what seems to be an impulsive reaction without rational thinking of what will happen if I get caught; one two three, I put my phone on record mode in the middle bookshelf between books of similar colours acting like my chameleons out of plain sight while praying I won't get busted over this, or even worse, run out of battery.

Told you it was a stupid idea. But it's not like I'm prepared for my aunt's sudden death and have a recorder ready with me now. And since my phone has a camera, I might as well get our faces too. Maybe it would help.

I then sit towards it so my cryptic countenance faces right at my little mischief, setting the witnesses' seating on purpose while waiting patiently until Detective Jevon comes. Besides, he has agreed for me to be interviewed first.

6

The Cryptic Ghost

The conversation between me and Detective Jevon ran better and quicker than I had expected; for some reason, I didn't feel nervous at all. In fact, I felt pumped and relaxed at the same time. Even stupid exams made me more nervous than this. This one, excited me somehow. Most likely because I've got nothing to hide in the first place. I was truly being honest with him throughout the entire process. It was like giving a super honest interview without any preparation or even the slightest expectation to begin with.

I imagined I was in one of those job interviews. If they asked me, "Why do you want to work with us, one of the biggest companies in the world?"; instead of triggering my nervous system, instead of giving some fake incredible answer, I'd say, "I actually never want to work here. Let's be honest; even your job sucks."

Only two consequences; either I walked out the door alone without a job or the interviewer came out of the building with me. Both options sound like a happy ending to me. That's how chill the interrogation process was for me.

Another thing about the interrogation; it opened my eyes to another revelation, a very sad one. I was so busy creating my own version of Aunt Petunia in my head that I never actually got to know her. What was in her head all this time? Somehow, I wish I would've got to know her better, not only to solve this case. I mean, she was, is, was; anyway, my family too.

Poor Uncle Gershom. He's now just sobbing quietly on his seat and can't even think to console Idonia who's sitting on his right. Poor Idonia. Mrs. Oriel next to her seems ready to embrace her at any given minute but she looks much more comfortable sitting by herself, untouched and unhugged by anyone. She's not crying, she's not smiling, and she's hardly shutting her eyes. She's just looking down her thighs and both her palms are pressing hard on them. Looking at her gives me a bit of distraction from my accidentally-spy gadget.

I'm still anxious about my phone though. Getting caught and everything, putting my phone in secret like that. I mean, it can fall at any given moment. But I'm more worried about the battery. I'd be heartbroken if it didn't get to record everything. I really hate to be left out in suspense.

Will I get caught? And if I do get caught, will I be put into jail? Sitting here and waiting are just supporting my overthinking. Not good. I can think of a thousand possibilities how it will just end up going very badly for me.

Still, this mystery gives me the thrill and excitement I think I've been looking for all my life. I don't think I'm smart enough to solve it, or can make any money out of this (lose money is more like it), but I know I won't be able to stop trying. For Aunt Petunia, for the truth, for the family, and for myself.

My interview went on pretty quick but the others seem to take longer than I've predicted. Poor Detective Jevon; he's now with my mom and he'll probably rule her out from being the culprit just so she can stop talking. Actually, while they're still in the reading room, I'd better be pulling a mobile phone out of her bag that she has asked me to hold on for her. Besides, I know they're going to be in there for an exceptionally long while. And my mom has probably about a dozen mobile phones of her own for God knows why, it's even harder to guess which one she won't notice if goes missing.

Bad thing is, usually on one of those days, she does realise if anything, even the littlest thing, is missing. My mom is quite sharp by nature. Still, I'm wishing that this night will be one of those nights she won't be, so I won't have to come back to the living room dealing with her making a big fuss about it, or her claiming that the killer might have taken it as if her phone - or any of her phones for that matter - had something important. And if it does happen and I can't explain where my mobile phone is, I'll be screwed. But I'd rather risk it, as always.

I probably shouldn't waste a lot of my time worrying about this. It's done anyway, what can I do? Goodness, even I make more sense out of me now, almost as if I had just been born to-day. My head is even clear enough to remember that the kitchen staff is probably next in line to be interrogated and that the bathroom excuse almost always works in any cases.

I'd better do it first then.

"Do you have a moment? I want to ask some questions, if you don't mind," I ask, after going straight to the kitchen instead of the bathroom.

Playing detective, I've been.

Before I realise the time, I've almost finished interviewing all the chefs, kitchen hands, waiters, and maids in the house. Everyone except one. I seem to be missing Mr. Catullus. No one has any idea where he is at the moment. He might be outside giving a statement to the police.

"There is certainly no garlic in any of the dishes," says one kitchen hand.

"No, Miss, not even the base stock. And even today, yesterday and the day before; never," another adjoins in response.

"Madame hated it, everybody knows," Monsieur Scerri adds. "She hated the idea of her breath smelling like an undrained mould, even in the sleight of wind. Madame wouldn't want to risk it even for a moment of pleasure in the mouth."

"What about the wine bottles? I heard they were displaced. Where were they?" Another kitchen staff brings up his deduction. I should ask later if he wants to be my partner in this.

"It was misplaced in the regular fridge, instead of the wine fridge," says Lothar.

By who? I wonder.

Rayner then politely jumps into the conversation, "This happened more often than you might have expected, Miss. They're clear though. We heard the investigators rumbling about no poison traces in any of the wine, but they still took them anyway as evidence. They mumbled something about confirmation testing, but I couldn't understand the rest. Good God, who could have done such a thing?"

This time Rayner doesn't act like a robot, at all. I secretly hope for the sake of his good-looking face that he's not the killer. But no one, not even him, can explain to me who misplaced the bottles. Rayner did imply that it didn't matter. Could it be...

Let's pause for a minute here, before I get more carried away.

Something about garlic smell with no garlic; I know I've read it somewhere, that it could be important. That garlic confirmation is actually all that I want to know, but it feels that I can get something else useful that's not garlic relevant, if I keep going. Besides, there's still one more thing I'm very curious about.

"By the way, what would it have been for dessert actually?"

"Peach Melba. Simply would have been the best dessert you would have ever tasted, Miss. A fresh peach boiled altogether with some vanilla pod and sugar, accompanied by some vanilla ice cream and raspberry coulis after being cooled down. Shame that we were being instructed not to serve any more food for the night. As you may already suspect, they still take into consideration the possibility that Madame Petunia might have been poisoned!"

Goodness, Peach Melba. Monsieur Scerri, you've done it again. By the sound of it, it'd have surely tasted so delicious in my mouth. Argh, dammit killer! Why tonight!

And also, poisoned?

I knew it! This may have been a murder indeed. Kind of hard to think that Aunt Petunia had any reason to end her own life. Plus, I heedlessly desire that there's a law where murderers get more time in jail for causing cancellation to a bloody delicious dessert being eaten due to the murder they've committed. What a waste. All these wasted Peach Melbas deserve some justice too!

As I'm walking back to the living room, I keep thinking. Is it possible that one of the nice people there I've just talked to, or more, might turn out to be the culprit? It seems very hard to believe. But if it's not, that can only mean one thing - one of us on the dinner table. It can't be...

But that would explain why they're only keeping us in this room being closely watched and not them. And this blurry police officer from my view that has been watching us right now, I realise as I've come back to my seat, it feels to me his cold eyes are only watching me and not them. My gut now tells me that at least one of them was listening when I talked to the staff. Is there something the officers already know about us that we don't?

More notably, what and where was even the poison?

These non-stop seemingly-unreasonable hypotheses keep popping up in my head now like a firing machine gun.

The time I was spending with the staff as if I was the younger Detective Jevon to them all is certainly not as boring as being in this waiting room. But I think I've heard enough information from them. The one that went on the longest was just them rumbling about some *ghost* going around the ceilings that they believe must be contributing to Aunt Petunia's death. The rest afterward was just repetitions to what I've witnessed with my own eyes, but in their own exaggerated versions. Explains to me why they mentioned 'the ghost'.

Albeit, I wish I'm smarter than this. In those books, the main characters always seem to be able to get a meaningful grasp of something that seems wrong even on their first hearing. Meanwhile, I've got nothing, and I've got no one I can think of as the killer; I'm always pushing myself hard this low.

Killing my time by doing these interviews quietly is definitely the right decision. Not that long after I came back, everyone has already been interviewed and it seems that we can all finally go home.

Oh! I think that's Detective Jevon, from far away. I hope he hasn't found out about my phone. Time for some excuse.

"Restroom!" I scream peculiarly in front of everyone.

I should've not screamed.
Big mistake.

Everybody's looking at me now while I'm running frantically. How can I get my phone back when I've brought along all this attention with me? Regardless, I'm still heading towards the reading room as quickly as a bolt to get my little spy gadget back.

Passing Detective Jevon safely clearly shows that he hasn't found out about it. I'm then walking backward towards the reading room door in which Detective Jevon's eyes are still looking at me from quite afar. He looks confused; and I, the only reason why he's confused, look even more confused.

I'm not sure if he's going to go after me inside. I think he is. I mean, pretty sure even he's aware now that I've been acting strange all night; so before he catches up, I quickly get inside, close the door, grab my phone up here and a random book down here, then get out. I haven't even got enough time to see the cover of the book. Because I was right, he did follow me.

"What were you doing here?"

He asks me just in front of the door, as I'm about to leave successfully.

Fortunately, my action was quicker than his. When I was still in the reading room, I could sense that his palm was on the knob about to twist it, but I wasn't that sure because I didn't hear anything louder than my own breathing and heart pounding. And he's panting too, like he was sprinting to bust me. He was in such a rush to get to where we both are now.

Don't know if it was instinct or age, but I was faster. Maybe I'm not as stupid as I thought I was. Tonight must be my night, but certainly not Aunt Petunia's; bless her soul.

But apparently, it turns out that I grabbed a classic erotic novel by accident, which I've never read in my life; though this seems like a good excuse to hide my preceding suspicious accounts of behaviour. The expression he has when he glances at the novel tells me that he has either read it or at least known a bit about it. His face clearly suggests to me that the book is quite *salacious* for anyone's taste.

"Is there a problem, Detective?" I act, as I gesture with both of my hands with the book to go behind my back in slow motion. My mobile phone is already inside my pocket.

"No wonder you ran. You know, I've almost thought the worst. You don't have to hide it anymore. You may go, but please, *choose your path carefully*."

Whatever that means. Maybe he has actually read the book. Is the book really that execrable though? Honestly, I don't even care right now. And I don't even think my excuse is actually that legitimate or even making any sense at all but, oh well, as long as I get away with it. All I really care about now is what this little gadget contains. Yes!

My heart cannot stop jumping from seeing what seems to be a successful five-hour recording, with one percent battery left, sigh. I'm holding my mobile phone tightly, more carefully than I ever did, even inside this car. Can't risk the phone to fall down anywhere, not even on my thighs.

My mom beside me doesn't look tired but she hardly checks what's inside her bag. She's just quiet and looks out the window, clearly with no view worth viewing. She's holding hands with my dad who's doing the same. I almost never see this side of them. I can even just put this liability back inside her bag now if I want to because they look way too sad to even notice. I feel bad that I still need to sneak into their room later when they're asleep; it doesn't feel as right anymore for a reason I can't explain. But I can't stop now!

Once I get into my bedroom and wash myself, I prepare everything in order. The photos in my mind, these interviews, everything. And no, I'm not going to sleep tonight because I don't think I can. Or maybe I will, at one point, fall asleep when I get to the part when my mom's being interviewed. Whatever it'll be, I just can't wait to start!

Here I am, will be spending the next five hours of my life, investigating.

7

~

Eleven Witnesses - 1/11

The video recording from my phone is four hours and fifty eight minutes long to be exact.

The first witness, **Miss Daedalia Pavirsia-Abernathy** - that's me.

You have no idea how many times I feel I want to skip my interview, but I think it's better not to leave anything out - just in case.

I can see from the footage that my long black hair is bouncing furiously as I rush to get to the seat, even striking my chubby stomach and slightly puncturing my olive skin onto the table side in the process. I was anxious that Detective Jevon would be coming in any time soon.

"Ouch!" I growl.

No wonder I smell a little blood, the wound is still here on my right arm.

Soon, Detective Jevon walks in along with the police officer who was desperate to send me away from Aunt Petunia's body. That officer was definitely not happy to see me again. His face looks so relieved when the detective tells him to stand by the door, not anywhere near me. He must have thought that I'm Detective Jevon's problem now, not his.

I notice that I'm just about the detective's neck. The man is definitely taller than average, but I remember thinking to myself in that room that he looked the shortest among the tallests, instead of being simply exceptionally tall. Is there even such a thing, shortest among the tallests? Nah, he's just very tall but not super tall, that's what I meant. Why did I have to make it so complicated to describe?

"Aunt Petunia went to the bathroom, I think, before she went back to the dining room. But I don't know which one."

"Peter, could you confirm if they've checked all the bathrooms too?"

Have I just said something useful there?

If Aunt Petunia did get poisoned by someone else, she might have touched something in the bathroom that could do the trick. That seems plausible.

As for the rest of my interview, I was just voicing out in all honesty all of my inner thoughts, as it appears. It's like watching a repetition, so boring. I've been yawning for about twenty times throughout watching the approximately twenty-minute footage I was interviewed. Meaning I probably yawn once every minute of that video length; my body is desperately urging me to let go and rest.

I'm now watching myself leave, then followed by the next witness. My mom. But guessing how long it'll take, I've made a decision to sleep first and continue watching it afterward. I don't want to fall asleep while in it and get busted with the illicit video, just in case my parents barge into my room unexpectedly to check if I'm still weird.

At least I've got the boring part out of the line - watching myself being interrogated.

8

~

Eleven Witnesses - 2/11

Morning. No, afternoon. Maybe almost evening.

The empty dinner table downstairs clearly shows that I've missed both my privilege for breakfast and lunch, so I go to the kitchen to get myself a late lunch that my maid has kindly treasured for me. She knows me too well, but maybe this is just what all maids do to all stay-at-home spoiled brats. They know us too well. I bring the food myself to my room just so she doesn't think less of what I already am.

Fresh-made linguini stirred with some garlic, anchovies, and broccoli florets. It'd have probably been better if there had been some chopped pork sausages snorkelling on the sauce pool too. Seems like a perfect meal to watch some murder interrogations, slurping on long al dentes while chewing some chopped heavy-salty sustenance.

The second witness, **Mrs. Eleanor Abernathy**, my mom.

I never realised how similar we actually look, until I see what I'm seeing. I bet she was (still is) prettier than me when she was my age. I get lost for a few seconds there, but I can't stop laughing as soon as I watch her monopolise almost the whole conversation and let the detective only speak about one to three words of his mind. He barely has any chance to ask questions, but then again, he doesn't need to. My mom is just talking like an endless waterfall with tears falling down her cheeks from time to time as she recalls her old and recent days with my late aunt that I had no idea about.

"She has, I mean had, not been feeling well lately. She told me it had been going on for about three months now, occasionally though. She also told me she had gone to Doctor Godric for medical advice many times but she seemed to be getting worse and worse.

As I was saying, we all go to him for any medical advice, and he's really good at treating us. But the way he talked after he had pronounced Petunia dead, I think he knows more than what he's telling us. Mind you, he's a very good doctor, but very mysterious too, we find.

Isn't it odd that she was just suddenly... like that... I couldn't believe it, that in just a minute... and did I mention to you about the wine being missing? I think I did, but maybe I haven't explained it in more detail before. So the wine was missing, and oh my–"

And blah blah blah.

I lose count on how many smirks and bursted laughs I've made watching my mom talking endlessly, leaving Detective Jevon speechless; and everytime he's about to say something, pretty sure to stop the interview, my mom cleverly distorts him with other topics that keep him interested. By the look on his face, he clearly suffers the fear of missing out on information that he just lets my mom continue her babbles. Information hoarders, both of them.

Where most people find interrogation and police officers rather intimidating, it looks like my mom is quite enjoying it too. She means well though, I'm sure, as it also seems that she doesn't want to leave any information behind that can possibly help solving the case. Actually, maybe she can be my partner in this case. Bad idea. Bad bad idea.

Speaking about some of the things she says, something is odd.

I now recall how Doctor Godric said, "I ... can't say for sure, until I get her to autopsy."

That must mean he really knows something. My mom's right.

Maybe he didn't say it because he didn't want to say the wrong thing if he ended up being wrong, but what if he's right? Most importantly, what is it that he's thinking of that he's not sure about, that an autopsy can confirm? I should've asked him straight away when I had the striking chance.

9

∿

Eleven Witnesses - 3/11

The third witness, **Sir Bartlett Pavirsia,** my dad.

Compared to my mom, my dad is definitely a lot quieter than her, but not until he speaks about the things that excite him. Although they're about the same height and appearance, my dad's clean face and stunning wardrobe is a complete opposite to Detective Jevon's rough and hairy mien; but they're like a yellow and green banana after about a few minutes talking to each other. You do learn something new everyday, especially when the source is this felonious.

"Petun... I mean, the victim... was sitting on the edge by the window. My daughter was next to her on the right, then my wife, then me, Godric, Halihan, my younger brother Gershom, Miss Decima, Lesley, Madame Hilda, Oriel, and poor little Idonia.

It is a very long table so my brother had to sit very far, across from his wife. Well, because they just always are, I mean, were. Except when it was only the three of them, I think they would not sit like tonight.

They loved each other very much, and Idonia's their treasure."

Detective Jevon only asks where my dad was sitting, like everybody else, but he instead lists all of the seatings in more detail. He's actually done quite a great job at it. He never talks that much when my mom's around, but when given the chance, I guess he has unconsciously picked up a thing or two after thirty years of marriage.

But if I think about the seating arrangement again, if they're considering the suspect being the nearest that could poison Aunt Petunia, aren't they being sensible if they're putting me as a single variable in the equation?

10

~

Eleven Witnesses - 4/11

The fourth witness, **Mr. Godric Simpkin**.

As he comes into the room, his diamond-shaped face looks quite more contrastingly crystal pale than the rest. I want to be convinced that's not the first dead body he's ever seen in his life as a doctor, but his face keeps suggesting otherwise. Based on what my mom said, he should have known if something was up, and it seems to me from his comportment that he definitely does.

"Did Mrs. Petunia ever come to you for medical advice these past few weeks?"

Detective Jevon is getting straight to the point, right on the bull's eye, not wasting any more time. Probably because he has already wasted a lot of his time interviewing my mom.

I'm still very curious about what Doctor Godric is about to

say as his lips are still as tight as a sealed jar. He looks like he's thinking a lot about what to answer while his hands just stack on top of his lap, still sweating like melting ice. I didn't know anyone could release that much water out of their body. And if I'm right, Detective Jevon is also getting more and more suspicious of him. For some reason, he doesn't even bother asking if Doctor Godric is doing alright.

"No."

That's it? It takes that long for him to respond and it's not even the truth.

The way Detective Jevon raises his shoulders just a bit to lean his back on the chair shows to me that he thinks he has found the culprit, at least guilty of lying.

"Are you sure? I'll give you a chance to change your answer."

As a consequence, Doctor Godric gulps heavily that he almost chokes on his own saliva. A busted group of sputum. It's quite funny to watch.

"As a matter of fact, yes; but it's just for simple consultation, nothing much."

"Then why did you lie?"

"I did not lie. I simply thought it was irrelevant to the case."

He did lie.

"What was her medical concern?"

"She was just tired, that's all. Some diarrhoea too so she had been losing a lot of weight. I think she was just under a lot of stress. I suggested that she should talk to a psychiatrist instead. Nothing that her circle of friends wouldn't know, I'm sure. But I'm afraid I can't disclose any further."

"Did she tell you why?"

"No, we are, I mean, we were just in a doctor-patient relationship. She never told me anything personal."

"Did you kill her?"

Wow, slow down Detective Jevon.

"I did not! How dare–"

"Then, why did you lie?"

"I've told you, and I was nervous, okay! I had seen her many times before, and even afterward, from time to time, so it was like losing a part... family member. But nothing more! Besides, how do you know she was murdered? She could have *poisoned* herself, for all we know. Oh, dear Petunia."

"I never said 'poisoned'."

And then Doctor Godric cries, and almost chokes again.

I've never seen him getting so emotional, ever, in my life. It seems that those tears are the key to unlocking his kind of self that talks non-stop, as he continues blabbering about the disturbing event; I'm getting sleepy. He didn't even look that emotional during the incident, so why now in the reading room?

"Definitely, poisoned. That smell of *garlic*... that was ... like *Cor*... actually, I'd much prefer for the autopsy to confirm, and I don't want the matter to raise assumptions among others."

These words suddenly stop my just-occured yawning. The sleepiness is probably due to my full stomach too as I've just finished my lunch. Weirdly, I don't need another portion this time.

The garlic smell, I did notice it too. But 'Cor'?

Now I slightly remember. In one of those books that I've

read, one of the characters that's poisoned has a garlic smell coming from his mouth.

It's a pity that even until Doctor Godric's interrogation ends, he doesn't disclose any possible name of the poison. The price I had to pay for going in one ear and out the other. More pity that I don't actually remember the name of the toxicant, not to mention which book it is. Long hours I spent in the bookstore and I didn't even buy the darned book.

11

∽

Eleven Witnesses - 5/11

The next witness, the fifth, **Sir Halihan Dunbar**.

"Before we start, I would like to make it very clear that I am not under your arrest, and your legal right to interrogate me passes down from my own consent. Thus, I am very much entitled to leave anytime I want."

He hasn't even sat down yet but his moving lips under his bright garage moustache establishing his right already completes the job beyond measure. His hands are moving in such a way much commonly gestured by a lawyer standing in court that he actually is.

He's looking abundantly fearless. He's casually caressing the front side of his red hair like it's vacation time and his expression as if he's just sitting by the bay. His nervous system must have been wrecked from all of those *Palais de Justice* courts. And he was probably the only one so far who already knew the drill, unlike the rest of us.

Now that I think about his occupation, I remember how I wanted to be a murder defence lawyer once, and how I miss my dearest friend Boudicca, whose occupation is twin to him and living my dream. But daddy convinced me that I'd get myself killed the second I started, that the murderer would get to me first even before I reached the court. I have this thing of getting into trouble. But I think daddy's right in a way, because no interest ever lasted that long with me, not even this.

"Do you mind?"

Sir Halihan talks about the cigarettes he has already lit, suggesting he's not taking no for an answer.

I strongly ponder if it's not just about the smokes; actually, he just wants to position his place in the room. In response, Detective Jevon, still acting polite, nods to the ruby head hesitantly just to indicate he's getting the message; he's expecting no quarrel.

"Who do you think would want to kill Mrs. Petunia?"

He takes his glasses out and answers, "No one."

"Let me change the question then. Who do you think will benefit the most from Mrs. Petunia's murder?"

"You call it a murder? I'd say it was a suicide."

"How so? And you haven't answered my question. Should I ask you this again in a different tune?"

"No need. My brain is perfectly capable of remembering. I'd say in this case, little Miss Idonia Pavirsia. Not that the information will be of any use to your investigation. And for what it's worth, the insurance claim only adds about one percent to what the family owns. Her death, in my personal opinion, only adds a million more tears to the family and not a penny more to the bank."

Poor little Idonia. I almost forgot about her.

She's still so little yet she already has to bear so much. I remember how her eyes were seemingly flooded with silent tears. She was speechless as she stood. She wouldn't want to talk to anybody afterward and came back straight to her room, until the police arrived. Her evident mourning somehow even more encourages me to find what lies beneath Aunt Petunia's death.

"Do *us* a little favour, won't you, Detective? Save Idonia's interview for last. The little girl has been going through so much, and seeing the victim die in front of her eyes like that."

"I'll see what I can do."

I strongly doubt that Detective Jevon will respect or do anything to grant Sir Halihan's favour after all that, but I think he's considering this one. I bet he thinks he'd be the devil himself not to compromise on this. He even granted my odd wish to be the first one to be interviewed, let alone for the sake of a little child in grief like Idonia.

Sir Halihan looks quite relieved when the detective nods lightly, seemingly conforming to his wish. He soon lets himself out after turning off his cigarette as if it has already fulfilled its sole purpose. I never knew he actually cares about Idonia that much.

Seeing the face of the next witness already entering the room, I'm quite sure that Detective Jevon's lung function will deteriorate in percentage fifty times more than the amount of smoke he's already got from Sir Halihan.

12

∽

Eleven Witnesses - 6/11

The sixth witness, the blowing-to-the-face smoker, **Miss Decima Somerset**.

She already blasts her smoke to poor Detective Jevon's face in the first few seconds her lower body touches the seat.

"I do not wish to stay any longer than ten minutes," she begins, even before her upper body is properly adjusting to the back of the chair. She then continues blowing her cigarette onto his face as a closing statement.

"Decima, why are you–"

"Why do you *choose* to be a police officer, *Detective*?"

She forcefully freezes the detective's question as if she already knows what he's going to say.

I can feel it in her eyes. There's a sense of urgency coming from her, that she feels the need to immediately put a stop to the question; whatever it takes, she won't let him finish the sentence.

Wait, do they already know each other?

"So this is how you want to play it? To act like you don't even know me?"

So they do know each other. Seriously?

And as the only response he gets is wordless air with hefty blow and stinky smoke, he hopelessly adds his part, "Alright, I believe, for the safety of the people, *Miss.*"

"Tsk, the people."

Then a prolonged silence follows the two souls obviously having some fiery affair in the past - a very bad one I presume. Don't tell me that perhaps they used to... date each other? I smell drama.

"And about Petunia, I think it's the husband."

Uncle Gershom? And I can feel that my eyes are getting wider than they usually are. Dad's brother? Really?

"Or the cheater; well, she had been cheating on him," she adds subsequently.

She responds simply with her no-bull attitude, implying no space between cold talks and elaboration. She's giving answers even before there's any question, at least the kind that seems to be related to the case.

"Do you know with whom?"

Instead of answering immediately, she instead touches her short hair that entwines just perfectly in the colour of a sunshine, maybe just to check if each hairline is still flawlessly curled to the light. She then changes her seating position, from crossing her right leg towards the door, to her left by the window. She takes a deep breath to inhale the sleeping nicotine, just to toss it out back in the air, and she does that repeatedly as before. She seems to be doing it on purpose to get on the detective's bootless nerve that, regardless, still looks suppressed by the charisma she possesses.

"Better talk to that two-faced old-bag Oriel. She knows a lot more than she should."

She now looks really satisfied saying it.

"I just, how to simply put it, do not care about others, or the safety of anyone other than myself, *Detective*," she continues, seemingly to respond to a different kind of matter.

The way she says 'Detective' to Detective Jevon is always with the same tone, unpleasantly smirked and conceited.

"To put it this way, she's a hypocrite. Too bad she's not smart enough to kill someone," she further reveals.

She obviously doesn't like Mrs. Oriel at all, but I thought she just hated everyone.

"You seem to not being fond of Mrs. Oriel for being 'two-faced', as you put it?"

"Everyone has two faces, *Detective*, maybe even more. But about that little old shrew, I just simply hate all of her faces," she adds more smirks and simpers all over the vocables.

"Just so you know, one cannot have that many check ups in a year," she leaves a hint before letting herself out of the door, but I think I get her point.

"You know, I always wonder what it feels like to... kill someone," she suddenly unleashes a calamitous parcel of words from the moving cavity of her face.

What comes next just doesn't seem PG-rated to thirsty striplings. She stops by the door and lowers her giant furry cardigan to reveal her naked left shoulder.

"You know, it's a shame a man like you chooses to be what you are, who you are, and... for the people. Sigh, such a waste of a good look," she says, and this time, in a much deeper voice.

"And oh my, look at the time, it's almost exactly ten minutes."

She winks at him before she disappears but then slams the door in what sounds like a vehement falling glacier of ice, followed by an establishment of a statue of a sitting man who might just be infatuated with the coquette, possibly all over again. I mean, he just turns extremely silent looking at the door, not even moving an inch.

Complicated woman, that one.

I'm a woman too but even I still don't understand Miss Decima. It's like seeing twelve different women in one body. She's this one book with all kinds of genres that just draws all types of readers liking the suspense.

With her cold yet inviting gestures, in addition to her abyssal voice and most of the detective's silent hill I see from the mountain back of his head, resulting in a plausible flirtation play; boy, it's intense. I bet it slips his mind for a long second there to forget about the case and rekindle the flame.

13

✋

Eleven Witnesses - 7/11

Detective Jevon's glare of total blankness is hurriedly stopped by the unyielding blaze of the seventh witness, **Mrs. Oriel Walmsley**.

It's her vastly brief encounter with the previous witness who calls hard on her with a dust of hatred and not hiding it in. She knows she's the spilled tea.

"I would never, in a million years, never!"

She immediately repels all the rotten-plum asseveration straight away.

Is Detective Jevon always going to directly ask if they're the killer as his way of doing things around here? An implication can be benevolent.

"Petunia was my best friend! I would never do anything to

hurt her. Not that I don't know who might be responsible. Decima, she's a devil, that one, let me tell you."

At least Miss Decima didn't accuse Mrs. Oriel of being the killer, although in a degrading kind of way. But if Miss Decima finds out about this, she might change her mind.

This gets me thinking; what is really going on between the two of them, Miss Decima and Mrs. Oriel? The age gap between them is quite substantial but the resentment charmed between the both of them seems to only be carved up by a bridge only one-inch away. They fight like girls in school, they hate each other but always hang out together anyway.

"Cheating? Well, all I can say is, *my dear friend Petunia* was not much of an angel herself, and to consider how many times I told her not to, as *kind and caring of me*, I myself strongly oppose her manner. I was not able to stop her from refraining her past youth glory to some... an extent. She was what people may call, *grimalkin*, but I *stuck* by her side always, officer. People keep saying to me that *I'm too good for her*, but I believe there is always good in people, no matter how evil of an appearance or performance someone shows; *I am just that kind of woman*."

"Well, from what you yourself said to me, 'stuck' seems to be the appropriate word for this."

"Officer, the living can no longer adhere to the well of the dead, can't they? I just want to speak the truth, help with the case as much as I can; that is for the killer to be found, that's all. Everything I said is to help with the investigation."

Some best friend she is, was. I almost vomit a few times hearing her speak.

In a rush of rounding gear, I simply shift my perspective against Mrs. Oriel, and a little bit towards Miss Decima somehow.

Mrs. Oriel always seemed caring towards Aunt Petunia; but watching the video, she just doesn't seem as authentic, as she strongly tries to show people. Compared to Miss Decima; I mean, surely her behaviour is awful, but she is *genuinely* dreadful at the very least. Unlike Mrs. Oriel who seems to be pretentiously nice. Either this or I'm just being captivated as well to the iniquitous charisma Miss Decima has allured every one of us into that makes us agree to her animus. All in all, maybe because I just never really talk to the spine-chilling Miss Decima in person. I haven't got the courage to.

"We all know it's the Doctor, officer, and I'm sure Gershom knows about it too," she moves on as her closing statement comes to an end.

14

⌇

Eleven Witnesses - 8/11

Detective Jevon's writing onto his tiny black notebook is abruptly stopped by the hasty attendance and outburst singing version of the greeting 'hello' by the one and only, with her classic mouse bun hairstyle mimicking a loudspeaker crown; the eighth witness, **Mrs. Lesley Peacock**.

Once upon a time, a blabbering mouth was opened.

"I'm sorry, detective; I seem to always unconsciously sing in a murder interview... or everywhere else. Not that I was consciously doing it on purpose when I came in, or that I've been in one before; but then I'd have said 'unconsciously' when I walked in, correct? Ah, but that would be incorrect.

Did I say 'murder'? Not that I already knew it was a murder. Was it even a murder? I don't even know now if it really is. I mean, the real murderer would have known it was indeed a murder; not that I am the murderer. God's zounds! No, I would not, I would never; no, I am not, Sir. Actually, have you asked me any questions? I seem to have forgotten what's just happened," she says it all with a bouncing smile around her lips' edges, moving from left to right then left again.

I almost think that she's exercising her lips while talking at the same time. Clearly she's nervous. She usually doesn't sing that much in a conversation.

I'm still not entirely sure if the singing entrance is an act of nervousness or a simple vain, though it seems to me that the plumpish female probably just wants the detective to admit her trophy voice as she walks into the room; not that it matters to the relevancy of the case though. I'm sounding more like her now; oh God, not good.

Unlike us, the other ten witnesses, Detective Jevon may not know yet about her opera days, which I'm sure she's going to imperfectly aimlessly mention without being asked.

"God's zounds! Did I just say God's zounds? Gosh, I can't seem to shake that Shakesperian literature from my head, my oeuvre days of singing opera to blame," she continues, now with moving lips to the front and back instead.

There it is, I smirk.

And what do I get from her long interview? Not much, other than what I already saw yesternight with my own eyes, the exaggerated version, and what I already know about her mastery of the glorious and carolling warble, the extra-exaggerated version. Her interview feels as long as an actual opera duration.

"Is Mr. Gershom ready? Send him in, Peter."

Detective Jevon cuts her very long story short impatiently; and for that I must thank you, Detective.

15

~

Eleven Witnesses - 9/11

Detective Jevon talks to the man on the door the second time; it's Peter, who looks sleepy but quickly disappears after the repeat of the short instruction. I hope he wasn't dreaming of choking me out the door.

Mr. Gershom Pavirsia, the ninth witness, shortly walks in.

My uncle's eyes are still sobbing tears, his mouth is shut tightly and trembling.

"She's gone," he mumbles deeply across his dumpy cheeks and body parts.

"She was always so cautious about how she looked, how skinny she had to be, even until the time of her death. My beautiful wife."

And everytime the detective asks him various questions repetitively, he answers indistinguishably, until...

"Think about your daughter."

"Who cares!" He answers shortly and differently this time, resulting in the widened eyes of the detective's; and so were mine, to his and my disbelief.

I've seen it with my own eyes. Idonia has been his pride and joy. He used to take her around and everywhere on his back. It was so adorable. Still, that doesn't avoid the fact that, to my sudden realisation, I haven't actually seen the same picturesque scenes for a while now. I assumed it was because of Idonia growing up and they were just temporarily growing apart. Never crossed my mind that Uncle Gershom just simply didn't care about her anymore. I mean, what kind of father would do such a thing?

"Don't you care about your late wife, Sir?"

"She's gone."

Another kind of question and back to the loop he is. I can perceive imperfectly from the back of the detective's head that he regrets asking the obvious slippery question.

"We are going to talk to your daughter, Sir, just to let you know."

"My daughter, hmph, do whatever you please with her," then Uncle Gershom goes to the wind from the closing door.

This is something, I can feel it.

There is something more to Aunt Petunia's death that is about Idonia.

16

🙰

Eleven Witnesses - 10/11

Painfully next, the tenth witness, the little **Miss Idonia Pavirsia**.

She was supposed to be the last one to be interviewed; but pretty sure from the previous conversation with Uncle Gershom, Detective Jevon had the same gut.

She comes in as if her bony posture is about to be hovered graciously by the tremendously hollowed hurricane of grief. She's still walking vastly strong towards the four-leg seat without any noise despite the metaphoric thunderstorm.

"I know it's hard to see something as terrifying as death right in front of you. It's even harder to talk about it; but could you let me know anything that I should know of, to help me find out about what really happened to your mother?"

"Anything at all," Detective Jevon adds.

The little girl keeps looking down at her swinging legs. The detective decides to wait patiently until she's ready to speak. She then looks at him and says nothing. I think that's her response.

"To save you the trouble, why don't you start by saying anything you'd like to say? Hmm? Anything at all."

I think Detective Jevon may be smiling there when saying that. I can feel the warmth in his tone.

"For instance, what do you want to be when you grow up?"

"Do I have to wait until I grow up to become a writer?"

I didn't know Idonia wants to be a writer, maybe she already is. I guess despite her quiet persona, she still wants her story to be heard. I wonder what kind of story she wants to share.

"Do you like to write?"

"No," she responds, this time with a shorter breath and an infalling tone at the end.

I'm confused.

So she doesn't want to be a writer? But she just said... not that it matters. I also don't think Detective Jevon takes it as if it's of any relevance to the case, so he decides to let it go. I guess the last thing he wants beyond her appearing agony is for her to say something she doesn't want to say in the first place.

"But, I like reading. I suppose writing is the only way to start. I want people to hear *my version* of the story."

Oh, I see now, sort of.

Afterward, there's a bit of silent tension between them. Like before. She doesn't look like she wants to talk or know what to say. Detective Jevon doesn't seem to know what to ask or even what to get from her, but I'm just assuming this from the back of his head.

"You know, you can talk to me about anything. It will help me a lot if you tell me anything you know; for instance, if anyone you know wants to hurt your mother, or you," and I can tell from his voice that he tries his best to smile while saying this.

"She's not my mommy," she gives a response while looking up, maybe at Detective Jevon's widened eyes. I'd imagine she sees straight to his two orbs, but then she looks down again.

"What do you mean?"

Silence is her response, until she stands; that is when noises start coming out of her again, deriving out of her footsteps.

Did she mean what she said, literally?

I try to get over every possibility in my head, but it stops as soon as another familiar lady comes into the room.

Her steps have never looked so heavy.

17

~

Eleven Witnesses - 11/11

"Please, Mrs," says Detective Jevon as he stands by the door welcoming the eleventh witness politely.

Last but not least, **Mrs. Hilda Johnson**.

"Madame," she replies quite gratingly with her fatuous French accent.

Sorry, I mean Madame Hilda Johnson.

Compared to the others before her, she looks the most terrified; I can't even tell if she's more sad or scared. I can see her eyes are starting to build reservoirs streaming down the furrows below, either from the death of Aunt Petunia or the pressure from being questioned. Maybe just both.

"The night has been terrible, officer. It could have not gone any worse than this, of sixty nine years of my life, and the scene will be on replay within my memory for many years onward. I am very well aware," she responds with trembling hands tapping on her thighs.

Poor Madame Hilda. I'm starting to feel sorry for her.

"How could anyone do such a thing? I may be old, officer, but I know it was a murder. I'm sure of it and willing to bet my life on it. As much as I don't want to think that the murderer could be any one of us dining on that table, I might have a bit of a clue.

Daedalia, that young woman, has been acting weird all night! There's no doubt in my mind she's capable of doing such a thing. I'm not quite sure why. Actually, I know. She crashed an excavator, officer, on purpose! Almost killed one or two souls, I heard.

Although, this kind of string happened before, long ago... Perhaps, the past is repeating itself. She reminds me a lot of... that clueless, reckless, ignorant, impulsive behaviour... *Cor*... No. I'm sorry, officer. I've been mumbling so foolishly."

Wait.
What? Me? The murderer?
ARE YOU JOKING, WOMAN?

I'm screaming at the video, hoping they could've heard me from a different time dimension, and those words would still be the exact same words I shouted the loudest in the room.

What an unexpected ending of recording, that I've earned myself a murder suspicion medal as a prize. I've been 'acting weird all night'; well, she got that part right. But, still! And I 'almost killed one or two souls'? Not one single soul was even in there when I crashed that excavator by mistake. I repeat, by mistake. As if I hadn't done my due diligence beforehand to make sure no one was inside when I rode it, which of course I had. And that's why no one was killed!

Argh, this damn woman! Just great, now Detective Jevon thinks I'm a killer. I can just kiss that recent fantasy of interning as a detective, goodbye.

I knew it! She is indeed the source of this exaggerated form of information. She must be the one that started that gossip about Miss Daedalia stabbing someone. I knew I could always smell that gossip scent from her moving lips, that old woman is always spitting dirt around wherever she goes. It's like she's got nothing better to do.

Although, I wish Detective Jevon would have asked her more about what she meant by that, the kind of past she was mumbling about. Why didn't he?

Still, no guarantee she wouldn't exaggerate the story.

Why am I being so emotional now?

I almost can't believe what I've just heard. I've never in my life ever imagined being in such a position. I know I'm not the murderer. She should say that instead about...

The real murderer.

Actually, how did the real culprit do it? And if I were the killer, how would have I done it? I start to wonder as both of my arms fly over to the back of my head at the top of my silky headrest.

Who is he? Or maybe, who is she?

Who... who... who...

18

❧

The Daedalian Wanderer

I walk through a familiar corridor with an unfamiliar breath of fresh air. No one is noticing. The whole schmear seems super-normal, unlike any other, and it's only because I know I went through everything and everyone before.

There I am, was, as I look right into the other-day me, un-noticing the present me that is looking at her like a bolt from the blue. That woman looking bored is in the middle of a grown-up conversation with Uncle Gershom, Mrs. Oriel, and Sir Halihan while she - me - is desiring to run away at the same time. Her plan will be fulfilled right about... now.

There I am again, as I see her - me - walking towards the kitchen.

My daedalian mind is consequently confused as to whether I should call her I or she, her or me; as opposed to my inevitable conviction to follow a peculiar territory, in addition to my augmented credence that this is all just a record my brain has perfectly kept intact, of all of my senses, without my immediate awareness.

So I naturally go the opposite way from where I, she - let me simply call her Daedalia from now on - walks to as my brain at the same time reconstructs the actual events moving forward. And this is how I see everything now, as if countless small puzzle pieces of a tide of events are putting themselves together, piece by piece, as I go. This is also when I realise that those scientific researches are right; that memory is not a process of taking files from the cabinet, it is rather convolutedly *reconstructive*.

I know what Daedalia is up to, but what I've not known yet is everyone else's. Beyond my reach as I realise the following, beyond my witness to what would be my memory, everyone and everything else has been frozen in time and place, except for me - the present me. So Daedalia was excluded from the equation of my exception.

My warm body is confusedly going around every one of the cold statues in this evening parlour where Daedalia runs away from. I sense the crowding sound from the kitchen is stronger than here, because that is what I actually heard in reality the other day. Not at all from this extensive room. If I had stayed here a bit longer that day, I would've been able to see clearer what the people were doing here, while snooping on their conversations along the way. Instead, these mannequins are all I've got.

There is my mom, as expected, in the enormous cushy circle

of seats, along with Aunt Petunia on her right, Miss Decima on the right edge of the sofa, Mrs. Lesley across them sitting comfortably, and Mrs. Oriel coming towards. I notice that she immediately separates herself from Uncle Gershom and Sir Halihan after Daedalia leaves, probably feeling left out. It's obvious she's heading towards the empty left side next to my mom. I don't know why they kept it empty in the first place. Why didn't Mrs. Decima just sit next to my mom instead of choosing the edge?

Looking to the other right side of the room, I can also see that my dad and Doctor Godric are walking towards where Daedalia left to join Uncle Gershom and Sir Halihan. They've probably been talking about how grateful my dad is for the study table Doctor Godric has suggested to him and his brother. The doctor successfully intermediated as a trendsetter by buying the wooden furniture beforehand and let the siblings know. His storytelling about the unique panic feature even managed to convince my best friend's dad to also get one of those. They oddly established the design as one of the greatest out there.

Thinking of my best friend, I haven't seen her for quite a while; Bou. Though knowing her, she could just barge in here any second now coming unannounced and annoy me. But the two of us were quite the dream team. We seemingly tell each other everything whenever we meet, but even she only knows the tip-of-the-iceberg part of me.

Back about the room, this has got me thinking, as I continue to wander around here. There are only two people left that

I haven't seen other than Daedalia whose intention is known to mind.

Where are Idonia and Madame Hilda?

Idonia; I don't have a clue, and where she was must have slipped through my eyes and ears that I can't see or hear her anywhere here.

Madame Hilda, that sneaky woman who accuses me of such a horrid act. Either the case is the same with Idonia or my brain grows hatred that it just chooses to eliminate any view of her. But I demand my brain to act without prejudice for the sake of my genuine curiosity and let her into my memory if she's deemed to be here in reality. However, she's still a no show.

That's right, I remember now.

Right after my interesting conversation with Monsieur Scerri in the kitchen, she surprises me not long after that; to verify this, I run to where Daedalia currently is.

"... *voilà*! Beautiful like a painting, no?"

I've arrived just in time as I hear Monsieur Scerri's chiming passionate words come to an end. Now I can see Madame Hilda walking towards me from a small corridor.

"So, Daedalia, what are your plans now, dear?"

Stop.

I command my brain to do as I say, and to obey me it chooses. Not because Madame Hilda is being *Madame Hilda*, but because I already know my response to her agog. I'm eager to know where she came from. This is probably where I need more time to think. So once more, everyone and everything stops in motion right in front of me. Don't know until when. Maybe until I unconsciously whisper to my brain to stop 'the stop'.

Rewind.

And my brain puts everything back to the only place she could've been before, with her statue right at the front of the small corridor. This is when it stops again.

I pass her presence and barely make it to the aisle without my back making body contact to her spine. There are only two rooms in the indoor passageway. The left one is a big pantry where they put everything else that is not in the kitchen. I must have been here before, at least once, and that is why I can see the interior clearly, except for the ingredients and some cutleries and...

Wait a minute, aren't these wine glasses? I didn't go in here then; but if I'm right, my brain is showing me that this is where the wine glasses have always been kept, even before. I can also see the wine shelf. Some of these holes are pretty lonely. I wonder if some of these empty sections are the home to the missing wine.

The right side is a small restroom instead. It says on the door. I've never gone inside this little lavatory because I'm just looking at an empty room where my encephalon currently draws a blank picture. This will matter if this is in fact the loo that Aunt Petunia went to before her return to the dining room or where Madame Hilda went into shortly before the dinner started, if she didn't suspiciously go to the other room; which reminds me–

Ding-a-ling ding-a-ling ding-a-ling.

Oh right, the dining room!

And it seems that everything is going back into motion now while I stare heavily at the bare restroom.

As I arrive in the dining room, all of these twelve chairs are already full and everything is happening the way I know. It's so funny though. Some of them are talking then stopping, then talking again, all in a not-so-random loop. I realise, this is because they're only moving when I did see or hear them that day, and so my brain only replays what I really witnessed.

Maybe my brain is not as stupid as I always thought.

Good job, hippocampus.

It takes less time than I expected to adapt to the unusual lags of movement as I wander around the table and observe them one by one the way I remember it. It appears that my memory function is at its best when I'm unconscious.

I'm walking around the area. Other than Aunt Petunia looking rather awful and ready to vomit at any time her pride allows, everyone is doing what I've anticipated.

Except, I realise two more things.

Mrs. Oriel seems to already be aware of Aunt Petunia's sickness symptom, but as she has not fully concluded her holy-great charity adventures in Croatia to the intrigued Madame Hilda and fascinated Mrs. Lesley, and as she has not yet succeeded to attract Miss Decima's very expensive attention, she ignores Aunt Petunia in the meantime. And to think that I thought she had only realised Aunt Petunia's odd behaviour right before she asked the question. I can't believe I'm saying this to myself, I seem to be more and more on the same page with Miss Decima.

Another, that weird gesture of that one particular person. Why is Doctor Godric almost throwing his empty glass of wine in the air soon after he checks on whether the glass is dirty? Is it really dusty on the inside? Why not just blow it? Or, does he know something?

Idonia, now that I can freely look at her for a longer time, seems to be an extremely shy girl. That's probably why she spends most of the night looking down her thighs and plates interchangeably more than everyone else's eyes, including her mother. Does she even notice her mother's condition? I bet she was hiding in her bedroom too all that time, presumably why I haven't seen her anywhere in my memory before here.

Now that I have all the time in the world to take a closer look at Idonia, is it just me or does she really look more alike to Sir Halihan than Uncle Gershom? Not just the red hair, but even the facial expression of the both of them is very peculiarly similar. On the other hand, between Idonia and Uncle Gershom? Not so much. And to add horribly to that, now I don't even think Idonia has any resemblance to Aunt Petunia that much. Is Idonia even their daughter? Maybe she really meant what she said to Detective Jevon.

Hold on. What am I thinking?

No one is ever even suspicious of Idonia not being Uncle Gershom and Aunt Petunia's biological daughter, so why should I? I even visited Aunt Petunia when she gave birth to Idonia. Even Doctor Godric was there, Mrs. Lesley and Mrs. Oriel too. The whole gang was there.

Am I starting to overthink, over-analyse, over-fantasize everything again?

I remember that time, my ex-colleagues laughing at me in the meeting room.

"You've been sleeping too much, you think you're still living in your dream," they said while laughing energetically like they were really needing the entertainment.

They were probably right, because why would I even think about incorporating a mind-bending theory, tested by that famous intelligence agency to a bunch of world-class caught criminals, to a selective group of innocent consumers as a way to try increasing the revenue by ninety percent? Just because I had just finished reading those recently-declassified documents. That was just stupid and creepy. Even more stupid because I actually said to them what was actually on my mind.

Good thing that 'I'm joking' excuse always seemed to work.

I can't seem to squeeze my circle small even when there are people around me; and that is what I have to cope with almost everyday, this feeling that I don't fit in.

I think better when I'm alone, far better when I'm asleep. Sometimes being around people is just slowing me down because they confuse me even more. Either I care too much about what they think so I just stay quiet, or I prove my strangeness by bursting my quirkiness out of the bubble.

I don't even think that I actually act on it on purpose. Like that work we did, I'm pretty sure that my brain was just completely bored, that I just had to come up with something unusual to keep myself amused. But I really couldn't think of anything else, so I think I was just simply stupid. In the end, my whimsical opinions were just included as contingencies to make the reports more entertaining. Basically a joke. At least I think I contributed enough colours to the table before I left. They said I was the first kind and hopefully the last. That excavator story ought to be told forever. I definitely left in style.

That time, I always thought of the most bizarre thing happening; from an insanely giant dinosaur in the shape of a rocking tree coming towards the window in the middle of a presentation, to an alien attack from the heavy rain when we were still in the meeting room. They were getting me out of my focus. In my head, they were more realistic than if I had to explain. But that might have been more interesting to watch - I think that's what I thought.

Only this time, someone is going to end up dead, for real, on this table. But it wasn't as fun for me when it happened. Despite the fact that I seemed to be having quite a lot of fun in the process, the whole ordeal of expecting to see someone on the verge of death right in front of me was even worse than what I imagined.

As the waiters come in to fulfil their obligations, I notice that the wine glasses that Lothar and Rayner are bringing are exactly in the same order as when they were in the pantry, judging by the edges of the silver trays. I don't know if that was part of the agreement here for them.

This has got me thinking again. What if the poison was poured down inside the wine glass? If the killer knows as much as I do of the sequence up to the seating orders, won't that be possible to know which wine glass is to meet Aunt Petunia's lips? But despite the slight differences, there were still two silver trays and the direction of which they were taking them out of the tray could be different from time to time. There had to be some chances that the designated poison didn't get to Aunt Petunia. Unless...

This notion is even so conspiring to me that I barely notice the smell of the Chicken Ballotine that passes through my nostril.

My wandering thoughts suddenly stop though, when Aunt Petunia eventually stands. I would follow her movement but I know it would lead to nowhere. Still, my last-minute decision naturally decides to catch up with her anyway to see what's left of her up to going to the unknown. Then I realise it isn't a good idea after all.

Fast forward, to skip the blankness that's in front of her, rush back I go to the dining table area; but then I change the acceleration of speed back to normal, while waiting for Aunt Petunia's *fresh* return. Fear of missing out, I suppose, and also to longer reminisce about the beauty of this Chicken Ballotine in front of me I can no longer taste.

The foreseen missing wines have finally arrived and everything is going as it was, right to the fall of the great socialite; except this time, I've got one or two more discernments.

Does Doctor Godric look quite in pain to me? Like he's holding on to a nausea in secret and about to lose his breath too, but not as much as Aunt Petunia's. This is when I recall, that he doesn't even look that good in that interview video; as I also bend down with Daedalia towards Aunt Petunia's body. That would also explain his excessive sweat.

Weirdly, as Idonia is willingly forced to leave the horrendous scene, I see her giving a bull's eye to Doctor Godric; no doubt, with her red eyes almost winningly in favour with the red planet, and her mouth tingling with a seemingly irritated numb jaw. All to support her perfectly contained nuclear-blow temper.

To be honest, I'm not sure if Doctor Godric even notices the little child's glare. And to be fair, I'm not entirely sure what that means. But, could it be, perhaps, that Doctor Godric...

"Garlic."

Daedalia doesn't say a word, neither do I; but I know better than anyone else that that's my own voice I've just heard. Perhaps that's my brain talking or my memory speaking. The voice of my thought, to be exact, the inner speech of my mind. This, though, is the first one of mine I've heard so far in this reverie.

"... so the substance, just to be revealed momentarily, does interfere with cellular longevity by inhibiting the pyruvate dehydrogenase complex, resulting in cellular apoptosis..."

This I suddenly hear in continuance with the same familiar womanly and sandy voice that's mine; the smell, the paper scent, my memory triggers in a loud voice as my head moves towards the sky.

"*...hepatic and renal impairment may also result...*"

As the book is read, which title I once forgot I've now recalled.

"*...where the victim's breath unveils the mysterious allium sativum smell amidst the non-existence of garlic in any of the dishes on this horizon...*"

The underrated novel 'Murderous Affair From a Distant Horizon'.

"*Ladies and gentleman, may I present to you the poison...*"

I remember now.

"*Arsenic.*"

There it is! That's the one!

I at once jump up to joy, ironically in front of the cold lying body.

"Daedalia."

Huh?

"Daedalia," once more and louder, as I hear my mom's voice obviously from the other realm of the world; in half of an instant amount of time too, I wake up from my stupor, with my body sandwiching between the bed and the blanket and my arms intersected against my upper stomach. As it turns out, I have been in such a posture all along.

The eidetic anamnesis I did not know I keep still, the rigorous episodic memories I did not perceive I carry unexplainably in my sleep; all is brought to life as I fall deeply into my reverie.

19

∿

The Funeral

Aunt Petunia's funeral.

I never thought I would get to live this day before going into my thirties. I falsely predicted that Uncle Gershom's eating habit would kill him first.

That little wide blot in life, death, where some wish to happen much later or never when living merrily; copiously opposed when survival is no difference to misery. As much as death itself is the end of one's every odyssey, there seems to be no closure for the grieving rest who is left behind, ever. If it at the slightest reaches to barely scratch the soul of a stranger; it always, at the very least, ensuingly flickers an inquiry to one's heart when it's their time to be up and where to go afterwards. Perhaps this is why the importance of faith is established.

I think of this as I hear the mortal voices singing heavenly in this mighty house of worship, and see the coffin where the cold body of a stranger with a very familiar face lies peacefully inside.

"Poisoned I heard, can you imagine?"

A female stranger I've never met before effortlessly whispered loudly behind me and disrupted my pointless inner thoughts.

"It's on the news," I listen further as I begin to wonder how far the news has prosperously gone. I care less about who she is or who the companion is.

"That's it, though. No more. They didn't even mention what kind of poison. I don't understand why the police are being so secretive about the details," she continues.

"For a reason, I bet. There must be a murder investigation," the other one finally replies. She sounds smarter.

"Usually, when they're onto something, they're more reluctant to spare the details, afraid to mess it up," the smarter one adds.

Honestly, I think her mind is on the right track.

That so-called *guilty knowledge information*. I believe that's what they call it in the books too, propounding only the killer should know of. The police are looking forward to using it as their secret weapon someday.

In response to them, I sway my head to the back just for a split second so there's no eye contact. I'm curious now to see what they look like, particularly the smarter one, which afterward stays blurry in my head. I think I was going too quickly.

Now, for the million dollar question in my head, how can I

get the information? Even after this funeral procession finishes and we're all going back to the mansion where the awful incident happened, this is all I can think about - how to snoop on the investigation details.

I find each one of the eleven witnesses, including me, all sitting here just like that day. This living room. It hasn't been that long before they announce the mansion clean, but it does feel like it's been ages ago to me.

I see Madame Hilda chooses to sit far away across from me, but perhaps that's coincidentally the only seat she manages to get on with her almost-mediaeval pace of a walk. But it's so obvious to me now that she thinks I'm evil enough to commit a second murder in her imagination. She doesn't even dare to stare right at me, unless when I look away.

Naturally, my wayward scheme appears as a substitute for her asseveration towards me. I go to the buffet section with her eyes following me. I take a cup of tea and a glass of juice. My idea is to give the leaf infusion to her and see her reaction drawn from it; just because I'm curious what she'll do, as suggested by my brain that's keen on an evil laugh at the moment, and my decision to humour me just a little.

"Would you care for a cup of tea, Madame Hilda? You look extremely fatigued," my other face cringes in secret.

"Oh, dear, you don't have to," as she pushes the cup gently towards my stomach.

In response, I bend my body down like a willow and whisper very quietly, "You don't have to worry, Madame. There's no poison inside or anything like that, unless you think I'm the *killer* by any chance?"

"Of course not, dddear, don't be ridddiculous," she quickly counters with agitation. "I would certainly ttthink that is aaany-one bbbut... yyyou."

Then she grabs the cup of tea from my hand like hers on an earthquake and pretends to drink it. I know she just lets the water slightly touch her upper lips but her mouth is not willing to take the rest.

"You are too kind, Madame," then I get back to my seat with a circling eye, knowing the truth, while she hurriedly puts the cup on the table to never be touched ever again.

It achieves nothing besides a bit of a fulfilled amusement within my own contentment and affirmation of the fact that what is said in front of me is not always mirrored when the side is reversed. This is what it feels like to know the truth about someone's own perception of you through the rearview looking glass without being noticed.

By the way, where's Idonia? I'm sure she was just here a few minutes ago, but she can't be seen anywhere now. Does anyone even notice?

"Mam, do you know where Idonia is?" I ask one of the ladies in wait; and if I'm granted access to her room where she might be, the trip will be my very first.

"You are too polite, Miss. Please call me Adelle, regardless of my older age."

As she shows me the way with her kind gestures and useful inputs, I thank her.

Along the way, I think of one more question that has been haunting me.

"Do you know which restroom Aunt Petunia went into before... you know... the very last one she went into?"

"She went upstairs while the others were looking for the wine, so I believe it must be the one in *her* bedroom."

"Her bedroom? What do you mean?"

"I mean, they have... had not been sleeping together for a while now, Miss... then, for a long time now... well, not because of regular events... a big fight, the biggest!"

My eyes are enlarged, widened to the biggest extent.

Not to mention that Adelle is just willing to spill out the details that easily, but I guess it's good for me.

"If Mrs. Petunia had not died, we all assume the only way would have only been through a divorce because they acted like there was no going back, unless in public."

Shocking. A completely new information.

It never occurred to me that the two were having problems, or at least that big of a fight. I thought they were quite inseparable. Even that night, they still were; well, looked like they were. I wonder what happened.

"Also Miss," and as she continues her conjecture in a whisper, I think to myself how lucky I am to run into her to ask questions as she is utterly willing to give all the answers out of her perspective. I'm positive she can get along really well with my mom.

"I don't think I'm supposed to say anything to anyone about this but," she adds hesitantly, "since you seem to be some sort of *detective* too the other night, I thought this would help with your investigation."

"What is it?" I reply like nothing affects me.

But I happily don't deny it when she calls me a 'detective'. It has rather pumped my red balloon up to the sky without force. Probably the best job title I've ever come across that resonates with me, but my level of confidence slaps me and doesn't even dare to call myself one.

"There... Well, there was actually another death here in this mansion.

Wait, what?

"Wilbert Cruikshank," Adelle whispers so softly.

"The poor old man was the gardener here. He... well... died... also here... about three months ago, in his sleep. It was declared a natural cause or some sort, Miss; but I was one of those who first found him, and I can't help but notice a bit of similarities between the two."

She then shows a picture of him when he was still a living man. Adelle takes it from her side pocket.

The gardener stands in the middle with the other few workers in the mansion. I can't tell if his awkward smile means he was just trying his best to smile just like the others or he was forced to smile. Both of his hands hide in his two side pockets. Who knows how long ago it was taken, as even Adelle looks kind of different there, younger.

The man has a memorable crooked face, with white forest beard and white long hair; everything as pale as an old man should be. With his white coat dress, he looks more like a refined scientist, as if he's almost too neat there, or even too smart. As she shows in the next photo, the man looks completely different, but as appropriate as a gardener dresses, just by a mere change of wardrobe. All messy of grounds with his dark blue planting suit.

"My grandmother died when she was sleeping too, you see; but the way she looked, and Mr. Wilbert, he looked nothing like my grandmother at all. It was just... not natural. My grandmother looked like she was dying in peace. Mr. Wilbert... there must be some sort of *malice*, Miss. My gut tells me so," she adds.

"You mean, he might be murdered? Poisoned?"

"I can't say for sure, Miss. Mind you, people like us; they might not even think it was worth their time to figure out the real cause of death, a completely different case when... if you don't mind me saying."

"No, not at all. But I understand what you mean. And I agree, that sounds completely unfair, Adelle."

"Thank you, Miss. If only they had done some sort of 'tupsy' like one of those on TV, maybe the case would have been different."

"You mean, autopsy?"

"My deep apology, Miss; but yes, that is the one. Poor Tamerlane, the poor old man's grandson. The little kid adored him very much, even more than his parents he's living with. Not to mention they do not have a lot to eat as well."

"You know him? The little kid?"

"Well yes, but not really. He used to come here very often to help his grandfather. My relationship with him is as far as bringing a glass of water out of pity whenever he comes to visit; not that he does, anymore."

"You saw his body, the poor old man. So, it was similar to Aunt Petunia's, you'd say? You're positive?"

"Maybe not a hundred percent, Miss; but yes, quite positive. Their expression, I glimpsed. I can never forget that. Forever imprinted in my mind, I must surrender."

"Who else knows about this?"

"You mean, about his death? The similarity?"

"Everything."

"I'm afraid it all stays in the house, Miss. Even if it gets out, I don't think anyone is interested to hear it. Anyone but you, Miss. I hope I'm right."

"You are. Thank you very much, Adelle. And please; anything else, don't hesitate to tell me straight away. Did you tell the police too about this?"

"None of us did, Miss. We were told specifically by Mr. Catullus not to. We the rest are all just the body, following the head, you see. But I presume the police already knows about this, Miss?"

"Well, I mean, they were in the same location–"

"It's definitely a murder, right, Miss?"

"I'm sorry, I don't know yet. It's still just my assumption."

"I see, Miss."

"My aunt... Do you think there's any chance it could be a suicide?"

"Well Miss, Madame had not been herself for a while. I thought everyone would have noticed it too."

"Oh yes, was it... since the fight, you said?"

"I think... I'm afraid so. Madame cannot sleep without a cup of chamomile tea every night ever since."

"Also, Miss," she continues, "Would you mind telling me if you've got anything new about Mr. Wilbert's death?"

"Oh?"

"It's just, I feel very sorry for his grandson. Poor Tamerlane."

"Oh yes, and poor Idonia too. I feel sorry for both of them."

"Well yes, Miss, but no offence. Miss Idonia, she has everything, more than enough to help with her grief. Tamerlane, even with the same age as Miss Idonia, still has to worry about what to eat for the day."

"And some nights, Miss," she adds, "then, always before the murder, there is this *spirit voice*," but then abruptly stops as soon as she sees Mr. Catullus; and he's watching us like a hawk, not far from where we're standing.

I almost thought I had seen the real ghost there.

"I'd better go, Miss," she hurriedly leaves my presence.

Something is odd.

What spirit voice? Sounds nonsense.
But, what if it's real?

20

The Emerald Green Spherule

Heading to Idonia's room.

The closer I get to her chamber, the slower the pace I bring to the floor.

I begin to ask myself the following questions. What is my real intention in the first place to find her? Caring about her? Curious of her hiding place, is it really the bedroom? Or should I ask more questions to the butlers and maids instead? Maybe they're a better use for my time.

But just before I change my mind, my body has already taken its seemingly rightful place in front of her room, knocking at her door.

Knock knock knock.

"Idonia?" I call her almost quietly.

There's no response. Perhaps I'm not being loud enough.

Instead of calling out her name again, I impolitely proceed to twist the knob to get myself private access to her boudoir.

There she is, as expected; but what she's doing is far beyond my expectation.

She's lying sideways by the entrance of a plenum space on the top of, not her bed, not the floor, a skyrising pale-coloured wardrobe that almost touches the ceiling. Her skinny body fits perfectly between the gaps. The handmade stair made out of different shapes of boxes from purchases of her high-end clothes seems to be the only way she was able to get to the top.

On her hand is, what I call in my head, an *emerald green spherule*. It's almost the same size and shape as a tennis ball with the colour slightly more mesmerising; basically, a shimmering-green plastic ball. From the sound of what she's currently doing to the ball, hitting it up and down to the ground perfectly, it seems to be the same weight as a tennis ball too.

May I say, what a skill she's got there. Even her one-second wandered eye variance established from my sudden arrival doesn't cause the ball to miss her palm as it soars to the sky with the help of gravity. The ball is perfectly captured by her grip even when she's looking at me.

"You play tennis?" I notice my voice sounds a bit different when I'm talking to her, sounding more considerate.

"No," she answers me with a heavy sigh instead.

What a stupid question, that's my fault.

"That's a nice green-looking bouncing little ball you've got there. Where did you get it?"

"Someone gave it to me."

"Oh, who was it?"

This time, she doesn't answer.

I guess I have to assume that Aunt Petunia gave it to her. Perhaps on her birthday, seeing how exquisite and unusual it is. As such, she doesn't feel like talking about it or even giving the slightest mention of her. Her eyes seem to confirm my hypothesis for me.

"Am I disturbing?" I ask in response to her inaudible words, as she shows no interest in mine.

I'm ready to leave if she finds me a bother.

Before she answers, she stops for a while instead of continuing throwing off the ball; then without looking at me again, she rises to my bait of words, "No."

A heavy sigh for myself there, but with a sense of relief; as I exhale this earthy, musky, sweet smell from her room diffuser. Apparently, I prefer to stay.

"What a bunch of storybooks you've got here."

"For references," she responds very shortly while slightly acting afresh, delaying a second on throwing off the ball.

"I think they're almost exactly the same as what I had when I was your age."

"So, you don't have them anymore?"

And once again, her ball-throwing systematic repetition stops before answering my question. I'm starting to know how to catch her full attention.

"Oh, I think I've still got them somewhere. I'll probably have to check the attic. If you want, I can even send them here."

"Send them? Like mail?"

"Umm, yeah, I guess so?"

I don't know why I said that. I think I confuse her just as much as she confuses me.

"You don't have to. You can just bring them out of the 'hide' and take a picture for me. I'll buy what I don't have. I'll throw away the ones I don't like anyway."

Ouch, I almost forgot how rich she is; well, technically.

"Speaking of 'hide', is this your hiding place?"

"Yes," she responds very plainly in a downward tone like she begins to feel tired of talking, or talking to me.

"Oh, I see."

"How long are you going to be here?"

Ouch again. I'm starting to regret ever coming here to check up on her.

I wonder what my response should be this time. Patience? Annoyed? Extremely annoyed? But she's just a kid anyway. So instead I respond, "Well, I can leave if you want. I just wanted to make sure that you're okay."

Then the ball stops taking the wing, immediately.

"You... worry about me?"

"Not just me, everyone too."

"I think it'd be just you."

I think my heart has just bloomed a rose, just one; and to think my heart can flutter this much from a kid's icy response, a ladylike child with a seemingly cold heart. It must have been the soft spot I've long had. Pretty sure I've just touched hers too because she starts to grow warm around me.

She gets down from her woody tower and we start talking. Favourite books, favourite cartoons. From here I realise that no matter how cold she is, she's just a kid. So I pretend that I was just a kid too. I momentarily reject the idea that I'm a grown up, it really helps with the conversation.

"You know, you're the first person to worry about me."

"I don't think so. I'm sure everyone in this house worries about you, even–"

I was going to say that Uncle Gershom was also worried about her. However, knowing what I think I know now, I think it's best not to.

"Anyway, Idonia, how are you feeling now?" I continue instead, and silence is her response.

"Do you..." I'm not sure if I'm making the right move, but here it goes, "... have any idea who might be responsible for your mot... I mean, Aunt Petunia's death?"

I don't know why, I was going to say 'mother'. I mean, how hard could it be to even spell the word; but somehow, my brain puts a brake on it. My gut tells me that it's not the right word to say, not today at least.

As I'm expecting her to say Doctor Godric's name the most, she slowly opens her mouth and pronounces, "*Hoggish.*"

That is not what I thought it would be as an answer, not even close.

"You mean, cheating? Greedy about men? You know she was cheating?"

She responds by taking her sight landing on the carpet below with her fingers dancing on the ground graciously. From that movement, I think I already know the answer. It's a 'yes'. She does know about it, somehow. Her strong eye focused on Doctor Godric the other night, so could it be...

"With... Doctor Godric?" I'm taking all my chances regardless of the outcome.

Confirmation to my hypothesis is what really matters to me now. Curious is what I am. Now that I think about it, maybe selfish is the right word. I'm being selfish.

"You know about the affair too?" She sounds shocked.

"I... I'm just guessing."

"How?"

And I thought I was the only one curious here.

"Well..."

Should I mention her brawny eyes on him the other night? Maybe not.

What else? What else? What else that I've got?

"He cries exceedingly during the interview with the police, which is very odd of him."

Hang on.

What have I just told her?

If she knows what she doesn't know, she'll respond with a sentence starting with 'how' again. Like how in the world could I know about it? Don't even get me started with the recording on my phone.

Just like that too, my heart is racing to the insanely-rapid beat in my chest. My brain is working overtime with exhaustion on another excuse; truth or lie, if she asks the 'how did you know' question once more. Please, don't.

"Oh yes, that's right, he did cry; so pathetic," she responds.

Every part of my soul in me cheers to where every breath in me pins my hopes on. Pressure's off. I can't believe my mind went blank over a little white lie to a child, and she's not even—

Hang on.

What did she just say?

21

~

Food for Thought

Click.

The sound of Idonia locking her door once I get myself out.
She doesn't really say much anymore afterward.

My steps continue to go down the whirling golden stairs.
Just below it is Uncle Gershom's study room. Shortly afterward,
I see my dear dad's brother coming towards it.

"Uncle!"

I don't intend to shout, but somehow my voice comes out
louder than I've expected.

"Oh, dear Daedalia. I didn't see you inside."

"I was from Idonia's bedroom."

"Oh," and he doesn't sound that pleasing or eager to know
what I was doing there.

"Do you want to know how she is?"

"Well, hmm, hmm," he doesn't sound so sure or care.

"She seems lonely," I'm not waiting any longer.

And as his response, he's uneasily bowing down his head, looking a bit left then a bit right. I don't know why but it almost looks like he's looking at his pants and wanting to know if there's more dust on his shoe that he needs his butler to clean, rather than learning about what his daughter really feels; all the while looking for the key to his study room.

"Are you okay, Uncle?" So I recoup his loss of awareness for a moment there.

"Oh, I am fine. Don't you worry, dear. You'd better go back to your parents and your brother."

"My brother? He's still in London."

"Oh yes, I mean your younger brother."

"Uncle, I only have one sibling - an older brother. I'm the youngest in my family."

I respond with a warming grin on my lips, just so he doesn't feel so bad about forgetting completely that he only has one nephew and niece from his only brother; as I see him stop turning the key, delaying on unlocking the door.

"Oh, of course. I am so sorry, my dear. My brain is just not with me at the moment."

"Uncle, are you sure you're really okay? Do you want me to call a doctor to check up on you?" I don't dare to say Doctor Godric's name.

"Oh, as a matter of fact, I'm going to meet him now, Doctor

Godric, in my study. Just to have a bit of discussion about, hmm, well, you know, something."

Does he really know everything? Maybe he's got a picture of the illicit affair and he wants to have that important conversation with that third-party in his marriage, right on the day of the burial ceremony of his former-beloved wife. I don't think this is a good idea if he already knows what's going on between Aunt Petunia and Doctor Godric. I mean, how can he not know? Even Idonia knows.

"Uncle..."

I follow him to the study room where he already is. I unintentionally glance at the entire area to take some time to think whether I should say what I think I should say or what I really want to say. Say it! Say that you absolutely think that this is a bad idea, worst!

"I'll be fine. Don't worry about me," and his smile when saying it is as shiny as sunshine.

"Just... I hope you're going to be alright, Uncle."

"Be good to your parents, they always worry about you. They love you so, dear," he decides to close the conversation with a piece of advice I always seem to forget.

He smiles again at me, takes the time to walk back to gently pat my head, then continues his journey to his seat in this study chamber. I ended up saying what I think I should instead.

"Daedalia, where have you been?"

My mom surprises me again just as soon as I cross the border-line of the living room door where the rest sits still. She always has a way of doing that.

"I've taken the courtesy to take all this food for you. I know these are your favourites. Here you've got the lamb chops, I got the biggest ones for you, and some turmeric rice, coconut spinach, prawn crackers, lots and lots of cucumbers because I want you to have as high of antioxidants as possible; also, cucumber has lots of vitamins so make sure you finish them all. Oh! I almost forgot, I also got you some potato chips on the sides, here. Actually, they're potato gems not chips, also..."

This time I glance at her and smile with a thousand reasons hearing her listing every food she has taken for me. It's like an entire set menu, this plate.

Soon after, we're both heading back to our seats. Just before my backside reaches the cushion, Doctor Godric has lifted up his to be able to stand properly. I'm correctly guessing that he's due on his private meeting with Uncle Gershom. His expression shows uncanny resemblance as usual, like calm before a thunderstorm; but his body manages to demonstrate otherwise, in particular, here now comes the hurricane.

As my thoughts are still revolving around various strings related to Aunt Petunia's murder, especially after hearing what Adelle has said to me, I immediately spade down my spoon onto some of these crispy gems.

"Oh!"

My mom lightly screams with her eyes seeing straight to mine. I'm confused.

"You don't take a moment anymore before eating? I notice. I thought you always had that long contemplation before filling your mouth full."

That is right.

Always, before eating. I usually describe them with various particular attributes up in my head; should've been such as this, about how this lamb was courteously braised to its supreme tenderness, or how the rice looks like they're invaded by the sunshine and hugged by all of these green leaves and kaleidoscopic stones surrounding it. I even often took the time to keep them in my memory gallery.

But no, not anymore. I guess my deep passion for appealing sustenance has shifted hastily and unanimously to the cold excitement of fathoming a discombobulated puzzle with countless branches. What a shift. Was I even that interested in food, or was I just, again, bored?

Dang-a-ling dang-a-ling dang-a-ling.

Similar but a completely different sound of bell, to put it in a way, and not as loud as the dinner bell I've heard many times. This one, it's my first time hearing it. If I'm not mistaken, this one sounds more like those coming from an electronic bell, set up to effortlessly sound like the rustic one.

Afterward, surprisingly, a scream of a man follows. Everyone races to the source where the constant voice is echoing; and in horror we all once again, in the very same abode, witness the view of another one's familiar face so terrible. Not sure if we can ever forget this too.

Uncle Gershom, sitting on his wooden throne in the study room with his back facing the window, with a dagger digs down on his forehead. The weapon seems to be retrieved from the closed glass credenza on our left, as one appears missing.

22

∽

The Missing Suspect

"Dear God," cries Mr. Catullus.

"Not again," Mrs. Oriel unintentionally catches on.

Thirty seconds have barely passed, obscurely not enough to get our attention away from the horror view; but Detective Jevon already pushes the front door not so politely, barging in uninvitedly, and in result widens his eyes to a disbelief that another case has been awaiting for his presence.

This gets me to think the next minute; what is he coming here for? The timing has never been more perfect. I don't think any of us has even thought of calling the police just yet.

As Detective Jevon reaches uncle with his nimble speed, he lands a couple of his fingers on his neck.

"He's gone," he confirms our utmost worry.

For the very first time, I hear my dad scream from the top of his lungs with a howling noise, scratching our empathy. Several of us even need to force our defence towards him to keep him out of the room and far from where his brother sits so helplessly. We know it's better for him this way. The best we can do right now is to keep his nightmare tonight as blurry as we can.

"My God, again?" Detective Jevon shakes his head and puts both his arms on the side.

After a short moment, he picks up his phone from his right pocket and calls for his team to arrive.

"Oh! It's Mr. Godric, Sir! He's the culprit! I saw it with my own eyes!" Catullus is shouting and it has never been louder.

Every one of us is shocked to the bone. Doctor Godric? Not to mention the hippocratic oath he has taken.

"His commute is only between his house and the hospital. We're basically the only family he's got. He isn't capable of doing such a thing!" Mrs. Oriel screams immediately in response. I wonder why she so quickly comes to his defence.

"Well, no offence; if he calls us his family too, that is. Also, since when do you really care that much about him? And why?" Miss Decima replies. My thoughts were exactly. Not that I spoke them out loud, I didn't dare as she did.

"I saw him running, just before I came in," Detective Jevon mumbles.

Well, if you saw him running, why didn't you catch him? Everyone knows a run after a scream is never good.

He quickly reaches his phone to climb up his ear while being back on the running race. I guess he's desperately calling for backup now, blaming himself for not stopping him earlier, or the butler for not being quick enough announcing this important news.

"No one gets near the body! No one touches anything! No one!" He screams at us repeatedly before he goes missing from our sight.

Great, at least this time I can save my scream for another time.

"Missing suspect, I repeat, missing suspect," his voice slowly disappears while trying to catch up with the physician who is supposed to save life, not costing one.

The decibel here counts down to zero, again. Everyone is once again petrified. I'm standing just between the line of the door to keep the barricade intact, hoping from here that my dad is going to survive the metaphoric burn from the pain. Mom's with him at least.

I must say, I'm impressed that everyone else is still waiting on the outside barrier of this door instead of leaving, quietly watching the scene like a painting with Uncle Gershom the only one in the picture. All remain speechless and eventually leave one by one. Seems they already know the drill now, not to touch the body or anything else in the room. Also, I think they're more scared of the detective now. He looked pretty pissed before running.

"Why is it Doctor Godric, you say?" My curiosity cooked into words.

"You see, Miss; as the bell rang, I immediately came to the room and found Mr. Godric in front of the desk. He ran as quickly as a bolt as soon as he realised I had opened the door. I even almost fell from the swing," his snow-coloured moustache follows his moving lips furiously, privately to my question from the others.

We're not far from the open door, and we're the only ones left here standing inside this room.

Mr. Catullus looks really old and fragile up close. He resembles a character fit for a story where the grandfather is weak and dying, but still in control. I don't think we've ever stood this near. I'm actually glad that he didn't fall from the runaway push, otherwise there could be two dead bodies today instead of one.

"I don't suppose the knife could come out of the ventilation above his head?" I speak as I look at the trifling entrance that barters the air between the expanse.

I adjust my wavering hypothesis to whatever fits my current vision. I actually didn't really mean to say it, but I ended up doing so as I was talking with myself out loud. This time, keeping my thoughts just to stay in my head is not as easy to do as before.

"That hole? No one can fit in there, Miss," he responds.

"But you didn't really see Doctor Godric stabbing Uncle Gershom, did you?"

"Not exactly... but he was the only one in the room! How could it not be him, Miss?"

Well, he's got a point, I must admit; unless, there was someone else here. But Doctor Godric was the only one seen coming and leaving the room. It's not like this murder is a work of a... ghost, right?

Somehow, I just have a feeling that he's not the man we're supposed to look for. I still don't understand why either, it's just my gut. I could definitely be wrong. It's not like I was never wrong before about anyone.

"I'm going to make sure no one enters the room then, while I wait for the police and forensic team," I continue my wisdom.

"You... you're not scared of the... the body, Miss?"

Good question.

No wonder I've been talking to him with his back facing the victim.

The scene is terrifying but I'm not quaking in my boots. My skates have perhaps kindly left me behind alone on this thin ice some time ago, slowly and with a trace. I'm tempted to get closer, but this far feels just enough for me, for now.

"Miss! Miss Idonia, please come back here!" Adelle screams and cries desperately.

The little girl is now standing just between the edge of the door, with her eyes wide open and her body frozen.

I almost forgot how small she is that I almost didn't see her. No tears on her face. Not sure exactly what she must be feeling right now from her vacant expression, but I trust that it's all tears in her mind and ripples in the heart.

As the view of Idonia gradually fades away from Adelle slowly but frantically drags her out of the room, I count down to the moment before the officers arrive. Won't be for another thirty seconds by now, they shouldn't be that far.

"No one called the police, right?" Just to make sure everyone is on the same page.

Everyone else remaining within my sight is either shaking their head or waiting for others to respond to my question instead. I guess we really need to just wait. I don't think the officers would take Detective Jevon's order lightly. As luck would have it, he just happened to be here, just in time.

Again, what a coincidence; but is it, though? If nothing is as pure as an accident, what does it imply by this then? This might just be another of my overthinking and ridiculousness; but think about it, Daedalia. Could there be some more connection to add, something that would or wouldn't have been there if the detective hadn't come as fast?

Shortly after my deep thinking, all the officers arrive to conduct their investigation. Not sure how long I was lost in the moment there.

All skins, floors, and walls in the catastrophic room are subject to the forensic team's testing. They gently escort every eyewitness out to the living room beforehand.

This room, again.

I'm back here to see how my dad is doing. It seems like he's calming down as my mother never leaves his side, not one second. Fortunately, with a seemingly no poison case, this time we can all still continue to take some food from the small buffet parlour nearby.

"Ouuuuuuch!"

Mrs. Lesley Peacock seems to be sitting on something, after she's back from grabbing more food from the buffet compartment. In response, she continuously sings in pain. This bit of unintended humour is probably what we all currently need.

"Oh, this is that *sleeping* pill! That kind, where you can basically do your normal activities while you're, well, asleep. You know, the one that workaholic people who don't sleep, well, take," she adds and acts like she knows the stuff, unless she really does.

"Those pills? Do you mean *focus* pills?" Sir Halihan tries to correct her, then shakes his head.

"Who does it belong to?" Miss Decima seems to be curious too.

"Simpkin... Godric... Oh! Doctor Godric!" Mrs. Lesley responds with a bit of an unmelodious scream this time.

She immediately runs outside to a police officer on duty to report it and goes with a smile, a proud one as she comes back saying, "I bet that could be important."

"How *impressive*," Miss Decima salutes her, but we all know she really means the other way around.

"What's going to happen to Idonia?" I ask the room almost full of the exact same witnesses that were here the night Aunt Petunia died, a small effort to detox the ambience.

Everyone seems to be looking at Sir Halihan.

That's right! I've just remembered. He's the godfather, for some reason. He doesn't seem to fit the father picture, if I'm being honest.

"I still find it suspicious why Petunia insisted on you being the guardian, you out of all people. You didn't sleep with her either, did you?" Miss Decima fires the bullets of words from her mouth. It's clearer to me now that it might just be her thing to always manage to do so.

Also, I feel Miss Decima and I are more and more being on the same page these days.

"Decima, how could you! She was eleven years his senior! Could you have a heart for a second, or could you not?" Mrs. Oriel tries to mend the bullet impact. I bet she's been waiting her whole life to say this.

"Not that it has stopped anyone before," Miss Decima responds merrily while launching another smoke out of her cannon mouth.

"I mean, think about it. Didn't this lawyer just get here thirteen years ago? What's his deal then?" She adds. Weirdly, she's looking right at me when saying it.

I admit she has some good points there. We probably have thought so too at some point in time, but we just let it slide. I now think of Miss Decima as a loudspeaker for the whispers in our mind, and heart.

Sir Halihan doesn't look happy about the accusation, but he shows no strength for a counter reaction. Very strange. Maybe he's just tired from the murder that just happened; but I still don't think he's the type to lose in an argument, especially when it comes to defeating Miss Decima in her repetitive cheeky wars. I'm somehow quite glad that she's won the war.

Still, something else just doesn't feel right to me, and my soul wants to know more. Naturally, my body brings me all the way back to where I was minutes ago. The crime scene.

"Miss Daedalia," the familiar sound of the detective who fails to catch the missing suspect, "I don't suppose you're planning to go back to the crime scene?"

"Oh, of course not," I tell a lie.

"I'm actually looking for you, *Officer*," supposedly another lie.

I'm not sure why I call him Officer instead of Detective this time. I think I was suddenly reminded by *that drama*, after *that war* recently that *that person* won.

"*Detective*; there's a difference," he quickly grasps on the humid interpretation that the amateur me seems to blow.

I didn't know it mattered that much. He almost reminds me of Madame Hilda.

"I'm sorry, *Detective*," I hurry in giving my response.

Now I sound like Miss Decima.

"Why did you come here coincidentally at the right time? I mean, really precisely. None of us even called yet."

"Good question. Even in my line of work, I know there's almost no such thing as a coincidence. But I must say, this time, it purely is."

"What was the reason you came here in the first place then?" I sound like I'm the one interrogating him now.

I'm giving off the Miss Decima vibe, but I do like this sudden confidence in me.

"Just... confirmation, and more investigation. We've found something odd you see, but it's not a subject to be disclosed yet."

"Is it about the... poison?"

"As a matter of fact, yes, but that is as far as I can tell you. Please go back to the living room. We will call every one of you one by one for questioning, again."

"Hold on, Detective!"

Another Daedalia that I've never heard before. I didn't know I had it in me to assert him. Am I dead while someone else is taking over my body? But I guess I really want to get more information so badly that my brain has decided to go with instinct and take the risk.

"Arsenic, isn't it, Detective? The poison?"

And just like that, his steps are stopped by his surprise towards my allegation. He doesn't look so good, but I don't look that fine either. I think we both seem pretty nervous now. Luckily, there isn't anybody else around us.

"How did you—"

"Garlic," I say confidently.

I think that's almost all the courage I've got left in me.

"I didn't say whether you are right or wrong."

"Your eyes said it; that it was arsenic."

To be honest, I never really get it when people say that they can see right through someone's eyes whether they're lying or not, or if someone's eyes perfectly look like the mother or the father, et cetera et cetera. Really, I never do. But I'm saying all this bunch of crap just to wing it; it's a bluff.

"I don't know where you were getting all of this; but dare I say this is logically making you more suspicious than the others, high enough to be a main suspect, to know such unreleased information."

Gulp, I almost forgot. That *guilty knowledge information*. That is actually a sensible accusation to follow.

"But —" my heart races to the endless speedy percussion inside as he cuts me short.

"Might it be you're that one murderer stupid enough to show off, or you're the smart kind and it is your intention for such so that it fulfils your getaway plan, or..."

Is there another possibility?

"That your deduction skill is one not to be underestimated."

Afterward, silence follows the air around us. Actually, it's not that silent; I'm hearing the crickets' sound. It's so awkward that we both just look the other way. One is regretting ever saying that, the other is wanting to scream a woo-hoo but doesn't want to show that she's that excited.

We bring our next steps silently to the reading room where the conversation between us goes more formally as we sit down face to face. Our seats are divided by the same table once more. Same place as before. Only this time, I didn't have to ask if I could go first.

A completely different atmosphere.

Detective Jevon asks me straight away what I know about the case, adding multiple times about the *benefit of the doubt*. Anyone here can still be the killer; he many times reassures that he'll never trust me to even be his unpaid assistant - at least I gave it a shot to ask. Having me being exposed to this sensitive information seems to be pointless after all.

By this time, I realise that I must do the following.

First is to fire away and hit as many clues as possible. Not just pointing out aimlessly, regardless of the more suspicion will be borned towards me. This is so that I can prove to him, more to myself, that I actually have what it takes more than what I thought I did. For the first time in my life, I think I can finally contribute something, something that really matters.

Second is to gain his trust by the only way I know how, not to lie to his face again. Not even white or grey lies or whatever, though maybe to an extent. I need to prove my trustworthiness, even though it's probably too late for me to do that; I will never tell him about the recording.

Last but not least, to try my best not to get in the way of the investigation; this is going to be hard. This is to manifest that I will be nothing but a gain to help crack the case.

Now, think again, Daedalia. What is more to add that is not far from crucial?

Then it hits me, where the poison was.

"Wine glass, correct?"

His eyes are broadened once more.

Am I... correct, again?

"This can also be anyone's lucky guess, really; but how did you come up with this, exactly?"

Frankly, I'm not a hundred percent sure when saying this, but there's still a basis to my bluff. I have sort of promised myself seconds ago to only speak of my deduction with only sensible grounds; I'm still not entirely sure how this works.

The practicality. It seems to me that the killer wants Aunt Petunia (and maybe Uncle Gershom too) to die with an audience; and with this, the choice of arsenic, the predicted time and place, they're all in the package. But why not the others? Why, a wine glass?

The regularity. It has slowly become apparent to me that

out of any object in the room, two are within the regime of habitual. The seating, which is always the same; if not, with at least a ninety nine percent chance of similarities (I can't always tell where the dusts are); and the wine glass order, at ninety. But why again, wine glass? Why not just the wine?

The target of course. Hell it would be to have one kill for a purpose, moreover for more than one without relevance.

Hang on a minute.

Something is hanging loose. There is more to this.

The sweat. The pale. It all makes sense if, "Doctor Godric's wine glass; perhaps, a trace of arsenic was found there too?"

I've got it!

I manage to have Detective Jevon move his hand from his chin to the table. His eyes are getting wider and wider too. I don't even care anymore if he thinks I'm the killer. I just want to know if I've actually got that right. I always have this one percent doubt even when I'm ninety nine percent sure; in effect, I need someone to tell me that I'm right so I no longer overemphasise that one percent as ninety.

"I swear though, I'm not the killer," I add, just in case, as I strongly believe that this one is worth the clarification the most. At least I still care about not being put in jail.

"Did you tell anyone else about this?"

"No."

"And did... anyone tell you this?"

"No one."

I can feel it.

I was right.

Confirmation to my hypothesis. There is no greater agony of anxiety than not knowing if what you think is right or wrong, more if there's no possible way to resolve it.

Regardless, I still don't know if I've managed to hit his trust circle and got in.

One thing for sure. Now that Doctor Godric is on the run, the greatest suspicion is conclusively pulled away from any of the remaining ten, as the mistrust ship currently harbours on the port of the missing suspect. Maybe in the process that boosts my confidence to speak up and lowers my overthink not to, in a way.

The betrayal.

The poison.

The meeting.

The runaway.

Why was his wine glass even poisoned?

Where are you, Doctor Godric?

And why are you running away? What really happened there?

Are you really the killer we've been looking for? Or are you just another victim?

Straight after, a never-before-seen image of a pair of razor-sharp eyes of him before running leaving the murder scene, suddenly appears. I'm not sure if this is real or it's just because I'm closing my eyes.

23

The Glass Cabinet

A whirling golden stairs, proud timber on the sides, inside is tough and bold. Still mesmerising though I've seen it quite often. The aesthetic human creation abraded by prodigious hands back in the old days, I believe, many centuries ago.

You, Daedalia, are strolling down the wooden steps like it's nothing but a mere alternative to get to the first level, besides jumping. You have neither the opportunity nor will to take a moment and appreciate its beauty.

From the left, Uncle Gershom - still very much alive - is walking towards what will be his murder scene. His mind is nowhere near clear, it's obvious from his face; his steps are undeniably accompanied with caution, they're heavy with doubts.

"Uncle!" I scream.

I have a choice to listen to the conversation that I already went through, but I'd rather refresh the body language that I didn't pay any attention to before, in the last meeting-him-alive jiffy.

"Oh, dear Daedalia. I didn't see you inside," he says, and with an astounding genuine shock; his mind has been preoccupied heavily by something dark enough that it's able to cover his eyes temporarily to his surroundings, near and far.

And, sweats? Why didn't I notice this earlier? Probably because there isn't as much there as that of Doctor Godric's that night of Aunt Petunia's murder. I have to get rather closer in proximity to even notice.

I've noticed something else. Throughout the rest of the conversation, he seems rather pale and confused. He also looks like he's holding onto something that he can't wait to burst out in the open. He has that expression where he needs to go to the bathroom at his earliest convenience but his body doesn't allow him to walk in there.

"Oh, I am fine. Don't you worry, dear."

No, you aren't, Uncle, and you aren't going to.

Anyway, moving on.

As I address his confusion correctly in regards to my big brother's current location, it also becomes more apparent to me that his confusion is mostly caused by something rather physical. Not so much of mentally at this point. The latter is rather the sequence. It's just very much unlike him.

Could it be... again?

"Uncle..."

The nerve skips a little as I've surprised myself by Daedalia's sudden barging into the previously closed study room.

Stop.

As everyone turns into sculptures and the scene into a temporary museum, I glance at the area as my heart tells me to.

No way.

The glass cabinet. It's already missing one dagger! And every bone in my body is convinced that it must be the same dagger which will succeedingly fly onto Uncle Gershom's forehead later on.

If that's the case then; Doctor Godric, the currently most-wanted man in this usually-peaceful town, couldn't have been able to use the knife because Uncle Gershom is pretty much still alive at this very moment I'm seeing.

That being said, so where? Under those circumstances, then who?

Did Doctor Godric perhaps already take it beforehand? But when? And how? It doesn't even make any sense. I saw him as he got up that evening. It didn't look like he was hiding a knife at all.

Most and foremost, why has the timing never been perfect to put himself right on time for the kill? Even if he wanted everyone to witness it again, just like Aunt Petunia's, why had it to be then? Did he really want to get caught that much? But if he did, why did he run away?

This thinking process loops me like a circle, trapping me inside.

But then again, why was a trace of arsenic even being found in his wine glass too that night?

Unless...

BEEP. BEEP. BEEP.

24

～

Bou's in Town

As brisk as the appearing waves by the sea, as alarming as a busted fire-alarm whose sound is no different to my phone ringing, and for every day too I always wonder why I haven't even changed the ringtone to something even more calming; I'm brought back to reality.

"I'm in town!"

It's Bou.

My best friend Boudicca, who lives a thousand miles from where I am, is calling out of the blue. She must be calling as soon as she lands. Sigh, she always does it so suddenly like this.

"Why are you calling me so early?"

"Early? It's already 12PM in the afternoon, you sleepyhead!" Her shout seems to be louder and louder as we both age;

therefore, I have to make justice for my ears by moving my phone astray.

"Why didn't you tell me beforehand? Sigh, you always do this!" I scream back with the words I already thought of.

I have this excitement that I can't wait to meet her, but also frustration as she always lets me know by surprise.

"You never reply to my message, or anyone, ever!"

Oh right, I almost forgot. That constant thing in my life I call one of my worst habits.

It's probably not that I don't have the time. Maybe it's more of a combination between my hopelessly incurable procrastination and everything else that is not texting, mostly spacing in and out of my reverie. I don't hate it - texting; but to put it in a way, I probably prefer talking to texting. It's the ultimate old-fashioned way. And when I say talking, I mean talking in my head.

Funny how sometimes I prefer the other way. I guess that's how I should be able to tell quicker if I really hate it somewhere. I simply become that person - you hate what you love, you love what you hate.

As I arrive at the agreed cafe for the very late brunch, the redhead woman of my age who vows to always curl the lower part of her hair for the public's view and not to ever have it shorter than her upper shoulder, can already be seen sitting by the window with her sweet latte on the rocks.

She, with her ultimate uphold for justice alongside her distinctive interest for waggish exertion, transfers into the expression of an embodied female chieftain. My best friend happens to be a promising attorney in one of the biggest law firms on the other side of the country. At least she uses her degree right, unlike *someone*.

Pretty sure we can't call it a brunch at this hour. It was all that we called for whenever it came to our very first meal of the day during our uni days, regardless of what the clock showed. I don't believe that the ritual is not what brought us together. Probably too, that's when my affectionate eyes and wandering mind for delicacy started. It was the only joyous thing for me as opposed to earning my useless degree.

We start the conversation with many stories from her end. Her occupation exposes her to many well-known murders stranger to town, most of which I may or may not have heard of; I keep up with the fiction more. She also shows me the list of the local news headlines she manages to skim every few minutes. It's not until I surprise her with my own stories in relation to the ongoing murder investigations, involving primarily my relatives and neighbours, when I saw those cases popped up from her list.

"I'll be damned. I still can't believe that you witnessed two murders and didn't even flinch!"

"Well, I flinched, just not out loud," I shape my humble defence; though, I might not call it as humble.

Bou then suddenly changes her voice from a humorous level to dead serious as I tell her all about these two murders. This must be how she constantly sounds at work.

"I must say, I thought the doctor would have been smarter

to at least remember about the *panic button*. Isn't that the same table our dad's got for their study room?

Reminds me of that one fine day recently. I went home, detached that bell and rang it from the garage, just to announce that I was in the house. Have I told you that story?"

She ends her share of memory guffawing proudly pretty badly.

She did worse than me. She almost killed her own family with a heart attack.

Boudicca Beischer, twenty five years old, yet her behaviour is sometimes still no different to those fifteen years younger.

I've seen her in a court once and it always amazes me how people can give a totally different impression if being separated from their duty; she is not excluded. Anyone at any age can see her true high intelligence just by hearing her relentlessly fighting with words in the courtroom. I believe it's just a matter of time before she gets herself poached into a high-profile case that turns into a documentary or based-on-real-life movie.

Most importantly, she's truly happy at what she's doing. She's having the best time of her life even when she's working. She's where she wants to be, she's where she's supposed to be, and she's damn good at it; something I've been searching for my whole life. As for me, when did that ever happen to me? Doesn't ring a bell.

Hang on.

"Wait, the bell is detachable? I didn't know that."

"Well, it's because you've never tried it. It's actually much harder to pull out than what you may think. Could even take a good one hour to crack if you don't want it to break. It's kind of stuck to the wood; but still, yeah, it's very much possible."

"Unless he didn't plan to... just a spur of the moment thing; or, he's not the killer."

"You think he's not?" She replies as she passes the question ball to me while still chewing the bacon in her mouth.

She always forgot that the school taught us to never speak while there's still food in our mouth. We hadn't been that close back then even though we were in the same class, not until when we went to the same uni, but I have a feeling she wasn't even following any rule then.

Whether I really think that Doctor Godric is not the killer; frankly, I don't know. Something just doesn't fit right into place, but I can't figure out yet what it is that makes me have that intuition, that he's not the culprit somehow. Maybe because it's too obvious? Unless, my intuition fools me. That wouldn't be the first.

Right, the bell.

That little panic button. I know now that it's more than possible to be detachable, as should have been clearly mentioned by the sales agent as one of its greatest features; probably my fault that I wasn't listening.

So what? Uncle Gershom may have rung it. But, what if?

I then proceed on telling her more to what's already

everything I know, everything I saw. My way of storytelling is greatly tested.

"So, do you think the bell was rung before or after my uncle was stabbed? Based on everything that I've told you."

"Well, I'm no forensic; but with a stab wound that deep, the way he sat looking up and hands on both sides, moreover to that particular side of the head, I'd say he wouldn't have had enough time to reach the bell afterward. I mean, from my cases so far, I've seen a shorter span of life just by stabbing something the size of a peanut to the head, imagine a dagger. But I heard some people did survive a gunshot with a bullet right through the skull.

I guess... it must have been before then? Assuming the bell was where it was initially put, all the way down there; but for his hand to be able to reach it even very slowly, you know, if he or someone else didn't move it anywhere else... unless... I doubt it, I really doubt it.

Actually, did you see where the bell was?"

Oh yes, I almost forgot. I didn't actually come very close to the body this time. I didn't even think of any bell. I've missed it, possibly again. Probably why I shouldn't overpride myself to play detective.

But if I still want to go on, maybe I can ask the butler, and the detective, if he's still willing to answer. But why do I have this feeling that I've probably seen it before?

What makes it worse for me is, I don't even think I would've surmised the idea of the bell if I hadn't spoken to Bou, plus her mentioning about the detachable feature of the bell. I was hoping I could solve these cases all on my own.

Daedalia, you bonehead. How could you even think that?

"I feel I want to come back to the mansion, to check some things out," actually just one thing - the bell. I hesitantly raise my voice to my long-distance confidante.

"Oh! I'll come too. Let's get the bill!"

"Wait, like now? You're okay with it?"

"You know how much I love mystery and how much you do too. This is so exciting! Should I just extend my holiday leave? Or should I just *crash* onto something? Oh wait, that was you!"

Surely, her dark humour never bores me. Before we realise, we're already running around the restaurant like an immature coterie of adults. We're completely forgetting how old we actually are. After a few circles, we're racing towards the counter before they all think we've been planning to run away from our obligation to pay for our food.

Before we know it too, we've arrived at the mansion. I may have driven too fast, I might even be speeding.

On the way though, I've been juggling my feelings about whether I should see Idonia.

The intense atmosphere here makes it feel like the awful incident just happened yesterday; well, it literally was. Not even a day, if we count in the twenty-four hour rule as the one day period. Thus, it explains the still-existing yellow lines.

"Blimey," Bou says, "If there was no police line, and you didn't tell me there was any murder here, I wouldn't have known."

Every word comes along with a honed pair of eyes that I think she genuinely means every alphabet combined.

The earliest part of her response is actually anticipated, but what comes after is not; not entirely at least. She thinks the murder scene looks a bit too clean to begin with. But perhaps she's seeing this merely objectively from her perspective as someone who didn't go through what I went through yesterday.

Still, I'm very impressed. First, her competence has just been demonstrated. Second, her bluffing skill, unlike any other; succeedingly we've passed the lemon bar in the pretence of her obligation as a defender representative abiding by the law. They seem to fear her more than their own team leader at this point, in which afterward we can barely hold our laughter to the disbelief of what she has just done notoriously in victory. I'm also glad that Detective Jevon is not here to watch.

"I still think it's too clean; you reckon, Dae?"

"I suppose. No signs of struggle you mean, Bou?"

"If the missing doctor was standing here, he would've to at least bend this much. It's quite an oversight. Therefore," as her fingers follow wherever the deduction of their master is going to, "this part down here should've been at least a little ruin, assuming he was in a hurry. Did you think they had cleaned the table?"

I'm trying to memorise if anything changes at all, if perhaps the CSIs clean them afterward or something; but the more the effort I put in, the more I'm sure that this is exactly the same as to what I saw yesterday when we all first saw the body. All neat and clean.

"You've got a point there, Bou," as I try to follow her mind after we agree that they've been too tidy before and after the murder. "So if we assume he went to either side, that would not be possible either, because uncle's body was facing the door; unless he quickly turned the chair back."

Subsequently, we try to move the grand wooden chair in the perception that it's the same to my uncle's weight; first, one by one; then, the both of us. It's too heavy.

It's more than possible for a man to turn it when it's empty; but with uncle's plumpish body on top of it, we come to a conclusion that the doctor wouldn't have had the time to do it, due to the bell. It could only be from across, because that would explain the body position more, but that's proven even harder.

"Hang on a minute," she suddenly surprises me as she goes under the table, "Where's the panic bell? Did they take the bell too?"

"It's not there? Or yeah, maybe they took it as evidence."

"Well, you might be right."

We're almost there to leave the table alone. My brain is moving faster than the speed of light but my body is idle instead. Soon after, Bou realises that I'm not following her footsteps to the cabinet.

"Bou, this got me thinking suddenly. If he did stab from across, shouldn't uncle be looking down, as in, his head should've been on the table? There wasn't even any blood there; I don't think there was, on this part here. He was looking up, you know."

"Good point. Now, I wonder too."

"Unless, "I continue as my view transits on to the miniature jail bars on the ceiling right on top of the chair, "the dagger flew onto his forehead, as if someone threw it towards uncle, like a *ghost*."

I probably shouldn't have said 'ghost' to a lawyer.

"Dae, one thing I've learned from my cases; sometimes it's best to take something at face value first, and save it for later when you have more. You know what I mean?"

I think so, so I nod. She sort of sounds like my ex-colleagues just now. Many times I've been told to be more realistic, than keeping my postulation in the fantasy land.

She disagrees about my flying-dagger theory, and yet she agrees on how it should have flown to uncle's forehead to have that fresh-body position. Now we learn that the stabbing is not as easily occurred the way we've assumed. Most and foremost, I've been learning a lot from her, a great deal. And I can tell that we're actually having fun. This crime scene becomes almost like our playground, sadly.

"The missing dagger, it's from down here?"

"Yes, that left bottom there."

"How tall is the doctor?"

"About one eighty. I'm not sure exactly."

"Well, okay. So he might've gone to this cabinet first while, or perhaps way before he went to talk to your uncle. He opened it slowly when no one was looking, then got the one from the bottom so he could easily hide it before action. Perhaps he hid it somewhere near the table, or the cabinet, so your uncle wouldn't be suspicious. This part makes sense to me."

It doesn't to me, though. I'm more than positive that her deduction will be no different to the police; but somehow, my feeling says something is weird about this. As highly sensible and probable that is, I don't think uncle would be that clueless, not realising one dagger was suddenly missing; but he did forget about my brother, so I may be wrong then.

But if the bell was just right there, down there below, Uncle Gershom could've had his hands slowly but ready to press it any moment he didn't feel at all safe. Then maybe, he might've had a chance. It wasn't like Doctor Godric to throw it immediately from the cabinet, unless he was some sort of knife-throwing champion. That wouldn't explain the standing dagger on his forehead and his body position, unless the dagger was really taken before uncle came in.

Oh right. My dream last night. Memory to be exact. If it wasn't due to some discombobulation between what I wanted to see and what I really did see, it really leads to every conclusion that Doctor Godric is conceivably not the killer. The knife was indeed already missing even before he came in. Again, if my dream and memory are not misleading me.

Unless, he did kill uncle and he took the dagger before he even came in, just like Bou said. Argh, back here again.

So many possibilities. I start to understand more about what she said, the face value advice thing Bou has mentioned.

Maybe I was just simply remembering it wrong. That wouldn't be a surprise, my brain really has its limit.

As we feel we've done everything we can in that room, also

the whole mansion, we politely refuse Mr. Catullus's kind offer to have our early dinner here.

"She's still in this mansion? She's not with Sir Halihan? And he's not even here? But she's still here? How can the police even allow that? And you all are still here too?" I'm still bursting with words, I'm obviously shocked and confused.

"I'm afraid he has requested us to take care of her on his behalf, at least just for the day. And he seemed to be in a hurry, Miss," Mr. Catullus replies.

I almost can't believe it. Now I think, for me and Bou to even be able to snuck in through the guards out there like this, it doesn't even feel that rewarding anymore; just because they think the killer is out there.

But what about the poison? Was there no poison in Uncle's case?

Poor little Miss Idonia. As fast as a rocket taking off, my decision is as quick too to check up on her immediately.

Knock. Knock. Knock.
Knock. Knock. Knock.
Knock. Knock. Knock.

She doesn't open the door even when my knuckles patiently thump on it with prolonged intervals. Mr. Catullus says she's inside though. Should I knock again? But she'll think I'm a nuisance if she just doesn't want to let me in. Regardless, I knock softly a couple times more. I guess I just want her to know that she's not alone.

As I don't want Bae to wait long downstairs, I decide to go down the whirling stairs once more and leave Idonia be.

"Where should we go for dinner? Must be something new, right? You choose!" I say enthusiastically as I'm tucking in my arms inside my coat's sleeves. I'm putting on the coat properly this time, ready to face the cold windy weather.

"I'm ready. Let's go, Bou!"

I see Bou just metres away outside the house from the entrance door, not responding to what should've been the most exciting thing she's heard all day. With confirmation that my voice was definitely loud enough to be heard, as I repeat them again in louder words, I begin to understand that it's rather because her mind has wandered to somewhere else.

Next to the mansion, right there on the left as there's where her head's facing towards.

I slowly walk to where she currently stands, without saying a word. I'm eager to see the distraction for myself. What is it that has successfully put a pause on her avidity for unexplored territory's delicate cuisine?

Police officers and the rest of the neighbourhood, along with everyone else in this mansion, seems to have migrated to the big house next door. Funny we never heard sirens or anything alike when we were inside. I wonder what is happening and when.

"There has been... another murder," Bae finally opens her mouth, as she scans the situation from afar.

Murder? Not even a possibility of accidental death or suicide? I wonder how she gets to that conclusion so quickly.

"This time, my gut tells me that," she continues.

Just like a telepathic sequence, she answers my question without me even asking.

We look at each other and it's just natural that our eyes lock in on the agreement to instead move our adventure next door. Gastronomy exploration will have to wait.

25

⁓

A Twisted Turn of Events

I can't believe that Bou's able to get us across the police line almost exactly the same way earlier, only with thousands of barriers more. Either her occupation or persuasion that is more I need to thank. Her prowess is proven unassailable on and off the record.

We unconsciously show our teeth bordered by the indentation of our lips, proud, but what we see afterward drives our beam away immediately as the horror strikes our view just with our early stand by the entrance's yellow line.

An old woman, still in her snow-coloured duster dress, hanging by a tail of twisted bronze devil's knobs off the second floor's dark-hazel fence right in the middle. The view is beyond enough of a scene to quickly regret our initial lack of sympathy as our curiosity pushed through our motivation atrociously to get through the crowds and officers more than the pity we had for the victim. Her body in a blink of an eye manages to steal the spotlight back even behind the crystal chandelier, centre part of the ceiling.

Her eyes.
Why are they still open?

As if the sight of her other features are not enough to blow everyone a good bleak of ice fumes, her eyes join in.

On my right seems to be the first eyewitness. Her black hair is swirling into a bundle and matches her floral dress perfectly. I know she found the victim by eavesdropping on her conversation with a face so familiar, Detective Jevon, again. I start to wonder if he's the only detective in town.

I won't be surprised if he suspects I may have something to do with this, and for that my consistent coincidental presence is to blame; much similar to his second visit, in my defence. The thing is, I don't even have the slightest idea who that woman is. This may be my greatest alibi in the meantime, not to mention I have a damn good lawyer standing right next to me who'll definitely and successfully vouch for my innocence.

Horrible. Who could've even done such a thing to a *loaded* old woman?

"Ghost! I tell you, ghost! Ever since *that thing* follows that little girl next door around," the eyewitness yells the preposterous culprit to blame, far from logical explanation.

That thing? What thing?

And, the little girl next door? Does she mean Idonia?

"Demon, I tell you! Crawling onto the platform too, perfect place for it like it's the perfect spot to wait for... for... for the right time... the right victim. He knows no one would dare to follow. Who knows who could be next! Who knows I could be next!" She adds hysterically.

I've never seen one as overwrought as she is, but she has a very solid reason to be.

More things I'm getting from eavesdropping. Her name is Avila. She's probably in her forties from her look; but she could also be in her thirties, providing today's fright has just caused her a decade of age progression. Apparently, she was supposed to take care of the victim when she arrived, like she usually did.

"Ghost, sigh, humour me," Boudicca mumbles and giggles just softly enough for me to hear, it's even followed by a snigger shortly after.

"Probably just the killer crawling through the vent," I then share my own version of an irrational explanation.

"Must be some roomy vent," she replies with a louder kind of giggles.

The stare of Avila arrives at us, noticing our disgraced burst of laugh, so we have our steps moving backward just a little bit far, away from her. She must be saying this to us in her head, something like, "Do you think this is funny, kids?"

"Do you reckon all of this happened just after we came in next door? There wasn't much of any time if it was, and there wasn't anyone here either when we arrived," I speak to Bou.

"Could be, or maybe she had just been found late."

"Right."

Just after that, Detective Jevon comes to greet us. Not peacefully, but with a face of a hurricane. Without any small talk, he mentions the ultimate irrelevancy of our attendance and asks us out as soon as his eyes are going to their next blink. However, Bou insists on us being filled in.

"Do you think she might have committed suicide?" Bou asks, demanding to get some kind of enlightenment of her cause of death; though my gut strongly says no, he won't get her the answer.

Instead of waiting for a response, I give in to the loud noise in my head by saying, "No," much to Detective Jevon and Bou's shock for my courtesy.

Then I add another, "I'm pretty sure she was murdered."

There is quite an awkward silence after that, majorly displayed by the two people in front of and next to me, until the detective decides to respond back to another of my odd behaviour.

"Why do you think that is?" He says.

To be honest, I'm not quite sure.

I certainly look very stupid now and I need to come up with an excuse for my impulsiveness, acting without thinking; the recklessness that has brought me here in this strange atmosphere, again and again. It'll be much easier to shrug my shoulders at fast speed and say that it's nothing, it's stupid, so I won't have to explain the complication that is inside my head that is also confusing me.

But I can't. I don't want to this time. So, I try to think, and hard. I'm pretty sure there's at least a couple of things that make me think this way. I just need to articulate my thoughts carefully and not let my emotions raise my low level of confidence.

"Well, to start," I then continue with a bit of silence again to buy my panicked brain more time, "I know that dress that the victim's wearing is not cheap. She may be the owner of this mansion, so why would she–"

"She is known for her acute depression," Detective Jevon cuts my response short.

Just like that, I realise I've given the wrong deduction. Even I can see that Bou is spiritually putting her right hand on her forehead. Stupid short moment of courage, I probably should've kept my mouth shut very tightly as usual.

What I don't expect is for him to say this afterward.

"Next?"

Does he want... another of my opinions?

I've never felt so miserably grateful in my life, as his inquisitiveness of me to perhaps prove myself (hopefully not as a killer) has come at a very bad time. I have no idea what else I can think of as an answer.

So I move my steps closer until my legs are just below the chandelier. My eyes lock hard on seeing just the dead body, but then my curiosity leads me to take the stairs up without any permission. Beyond my expectation, the detective tells the other officers that it's okay for me to get closer.

Perspiration. No doubt.

I'm having a better view of the back of her head from here,

but I think I don't want to take as far as taking a closer look at her red watery eyes for the sake of my better-sleep tonight.

This knot, these knots actually, as I touch the weird dark coloured rope, they look and smell weird too. So I repose my hands with an imaginary rope in the air, just to have a better picture of how it was constructed. May I say that whoever completed the knot was doing a very very very bad job. Even an amateur like me can tell that this looks too simple, yet at the same time, too cumbersome with so many multiples at the end of it. As if the killer was imagining tying his or her shoelace and subsequently doing it repetitively to make sure the rope didn't break. And if it wasn't for the strength of the thread, the body would've just fallen onto the ground. So why did the killer choose this method in the first place? Why forced it to have her hung?

Too clean, too. No poo, no pee, or anything that I can see from the lower part of her dress; as I let my head sneak in between the bars of the fence, just so I can see them clearly. Did she die before she even got on the rope? So how could the killer get her here so willingly?

So I proceed to unconsciously wear a glove given to me by someone behind me (I don't care who that is at the moment) and gently touch her hair. I want to see if she was hit in the head. No, though. There isn't any blood. Was she perhaps being drugged first?

"Good, for now," the detective's voice suddenly transports to behind me without me noticing; I can tell now that he gave me the glove.

As my view goes back to near the entrance door downstairs

where my best friend's still standing looking at me like she's seeing a totally familiar stranger, I accidentally hit my head hard right against the top of the gap, amusing anyone who sees.

"What do you mean?"

I ask him while patting myself on the head from the impact; it still hurts like crazy.

"I know what you're thinking, by seeing what you're doing," he replies.

"She died hours ago, probably after midnight or dawn, and there was no sign of blunt force trauma, so the killer must have drugged her first then brought her here," he surprisingly shares the information to me.

"Why are you telling me all this?"

"Just growing a little bit of faith in you."

"As in?"

I'm totally confused by his twisted turn of behaviour.

"That you're innocent."

Of course I am! About time my strange apprehension is seen as a pure growing attraction to solving the case; but I still can't help but ask, "Why?"

"Well, you're either a stupid killer or a complete innocent. But for now, my gut tells me to believe in you. Now, tell me in exact words everything you think you see."

There it is again the wonderful word I hear, 'gut'.

So I do, without leaving everything, even up to the point where I think she might have been drugged with arsenic too; though this can't be confirmed until she lies on the autopsy table. And for the first time in my life too, I feel that I might have a shot here, to be better than what I expected, and to have a better chance in solving the crime. We no doubt come to the agreement that the killer is the same.

I tell him about the missing knife too, and the absence of the bell, also the regularity of the wine glass placement. Even in repeat of everything I've already told him the other day. All except the hidden video, of course. By doing this, I feel extremely good and safe, also exceedingly bad for forgetting that we've been talking for the duration of a train getting from its first station to its final destination, while leaving Bou downstairs talking to Avila, the carer. I'm pretty sure everything they're talking about, I will know very soon.

"If you come to the station, ask for me," Detective Jevon says as we part.

Bou and I head to my car without her saying a word to me. She's doing that while looking at me, then shaking her head, then looking at me again, then shaking her head again. As we're now sitting comfortably inside, I'm not turning the engine straight away. Instead, I'm looking at her while she's looking at the dashboard. I think she's still trying to get her head around it and cook some words.

"I've never seen you so... so... so... and how come you were never helpful when we played escape room with the others?"

I laugh at her question. I know perfectly what she means; but to be honest, I have absolutely no clue. I'd ask myself the same question over and over again. Why did I always act stupid compared to now?

"If you had seen what I saw upstairs there, and the day before, and before, and before again; I think you would've thought the same thing too, Bou. I'm sure," I reply in defence of my famous slow-witted recognition, as I never really feel comfortable with even the side of the spotlight of a greater intelligence.

Bou and I, we now talk endlessly about what we could've been. If she were to leave her rising attorney career and instead pursue her other dream to breed as many Siberian huskies as she could for a living, or if I became a detective instead, what would our life have stored in place for us next then?

The question of why I really crashed that excavator keeps arising too. Then again, we've never really come up with a definite answer.

The next thing we know, Bou receives an urgent call from her office, miles away from here in Willowdale, asking for her immediate end of her current holiday leave for this. She almost throws her phone to my dashboard before being able to pull herself together to respond "yes" politely. When duty always calls, there's never a holiday.

I was starting to think how fun it would be if Bou was here too, in this town. Solving crimes together, and with her undoubtedly high intelligent brain and my unclear level of intelligence combined, I'm sure we'll be able to catch the killer in no time. However, since seemingly her career now solely depends on proving the senator's innocence over his mistress' murder, she has no choice but to bring forward the case as priority.

Goodbye, Bou. I have no doubt I'll be seeing your proud face all covered with victory very soon. I'll be hearing all about it on your next visit here.

The next thing I know, I wake up the next day all by myself, thinking about what I should do today. But I think I've already got a bit of a clue where I'm going.

26

An Unexpected Friend

The art gallery.

I stand by the moving blue-to-grey wave display right in the middle. I have no idea what this exhibition means but it somehow manages to attract my steps to unconsciously sink on the sand in front of it.

To my deep surprise, I can't help but notice a similar physiognomy sitting on a fake beach bench across. Alone, with her signature smoke cloud making the empty space next to her a dangerous territory no one really dares to enter. Her fashion statement does say 'I dare you to come close' but her smoke pattern suggests 'You'll be dead if you dare'.

I have my doubts whether to say hi to Miss Decima or not, just out of courtesy, but I also can't stop wondering what she's doing here. Maybe she's bored too. Thinking that the fumes she exhales will do me no good, I try to change my course of direction. That's until I hear her screaming with a sure smile afterward, what I have myself shouted before.

"STOP! EVERYONE, DON'T TOUCH ANYTHING!"

Much to the surprise of every person in the same room who immediately stares at her and stops whatever they were doing. They're all wondering if she was screaming at them, mere stranger to stranger, but I know better that it was directed to me. I think she indirectly asks me to sit with her. Sigh. Clearly she has no bashful vein as she appears totally unbothered by the confusion of her surroundings. Apparently that scream of mine that night made quite an impression on her for her to remember every word and repeat the sentence without any flaw, even down to the tone I put out.

"You know what's the current similarity between us?" She fires the hard question towards me. I have the choice to either be polite or to be myself when responding.

I secretly wish there isn't.

"That we have no idea why we're here?" I choose to be polite.

She laughs at my response, and to tell myself the truth, it's the most genuine reaction of hers that I've ever seen in my entire life. And this is actually the first time we have an actual conversation, just the two of us.

"All that right answer apart, that we become our better self when we're alone."

Her additional statement surprises me, but I have no reason to disagree. This leads to a serious silence between us, but I realise it's now my turn to turn the atmosphere around.

"Oh! That reminds me of another, that we're both single," I say in the hope of seeing another guffaw of her, or that I secretly desire she's going to spill the beans about what's really going on between her and Detective Jevon.

This time she stares with her sunglasses towards my eyes and corrects me, "That we *choose* to be single; there's a difference," but then she smiles again as her fingers lift the two pairs of black mirrors just a little, maybe to show me the point by gesture.

"How old were you?"

Ask anyone this question and they won't probably be able to guess what she means; but miraculously, by some deep telepathy connections we appear to form speedily (I'm not sure since when), I immediately know exactly what she means.

"Twenty two, one month before my graduation," is my answer.

"Twenty two, one week after my graduation," and for that she replies.

I guess we're not that different after all.

"It's always around that time that you know, when it's a bit too late. I guess that's the beauty of realising you're living and leaving someone else's expectation," she adds; but the way she says it, it's like she's talking to herself rather than to me.

We have deep and long conversations about the fake waves meeting the foreign shore afterward, the changing colour as they move back and forth, becoming one in perpetuity. So this is why we feel so strongly about the waves, as we eventually realise that we've seen ourselves as the shore.

In my sudden revelation, we both share quite similar views, but she doesn't seem so bombshelled by that. It's like she's always known we would get along if given the chance, not sure since when; and yet I was growing an unreasonable hatred towards her over only her selfish smoke act where in fact, this behaviour of her doesn't seem without a valid reason after all, as she stops blowing the smoke from the moment our body becomes neighbours.

Our discussion doesn't stop with the waves though. We share stories in the most cryptic ways. Some that I'm telling her are actually mine, just because I have a feeling she's doing the same. For us, and just us, we can let them out more this way. At this moment, we think of each other as one soul combined.

We never speak of any names, but I think I know one of the people in one of her 'coded stories'; just one, a guy. Although, I'm still not entirely sure. Heck, I'm still not even sure if confirming the name is the right move to do now. In my view, her response can still be any of the four seasons at every ticking second.

Before I know it, I drive my car to her mansion to have our lunch together; we can't seem to stop telling stories.

Our first lunch.
My first visit to my imaginary enemy's habitual place.

Even prior to having the chance to come in, I can already

imagine how hot the large house would be in summer, when the air conditioner is not on, and with all of these modern glasses attached to the whole structure of the house. All these giant mirrors, they don't show what the inside looks like.

But somehow, her house reminds me of her daily outfits; where glamour defeats comfort and enigma hides the purpose. The residence's elegance doesn't stop outside, even when it's so completely different in a way; but the paramount is where the inside is. With lots of magical-landscape paintings and velvet materials, I feel like I've brought myself into the most cinematic dark-fantasy book ever made into a home. Now, I can't wait to see her library. No wonder her ancestors started what eventually is the biggest publishing company today. I guess it has always been in her genes.

"Is that noisy sound from the vent still going on?" She asks one of her maids as we're sitting down on the grand dining chairs.

"Yes, Miss, but it's just a hole in the wind. The technician said so. Nothing to worry about."

"Thank you Katherine. Hole in the wind, whatever that means," and I notice that somehow the tone in her voice is so much different than her usual ones, almost like mine.

Afternoon becomes evening, evening turns to dark. After a few hours later, she has easily become one of the closest people I've known in this neighbourhood, as I am probably too - to her. We're bonding seemingly without any concrete reason. I've found this wonderful new friendship of ours, though it's formed quickly, to be beautiful and oddly precious. If she's playing an actress all this short time, she's doing a very good job at it.

Regardless, I'm still at my very best to be cautious not to spill anything that might benefit her if she were the killer, just in case. But I still don't mind her company. It's been a long time since the last time I met anyone as twin to me as her, if not the first time.

"I hope it's Oriel, I think it's her; and if it's her, I'm so ready for her if she's coming for me," she replies as our current discussion shifts in relevance to the murders.

"I thought you said it was the husband."

"And when did I say that?"

OH NO!

Why did I say that? I'm completely losing it right now. I was getting too comfortable. I said the wrong choice of words, totally. This is not good. If she has only said that once, in the interview, and she remembers, I'm so screwed. So I reply with the only kind of response I know best, diverting the question hoping she won't enquire further information, and act like I don't know anything. Besides, acting stupid is what I do best.

"And why Mrs. Oriel?" I ask while taking cover with my forks and knife dissecting the gems of the deep-fried plant on the plate and appearing as calm as the beach before a possible tsunami.

There's no fear in her words, but there's no doubt anger in her eyes. As it appears, she has been surrounded and hurt by those Mrs. Oriel alike, that she just "cannot stand even one more of them again, ever," she speaks with implied punctuation.

I can forever relate to that.

"I'm glad you seem to enjoy your food. You don't appear to think that I've *poisoned* them."

As a result, I burst some of the potatoes out onto the plate. Later, it becomes obvious that she's just joking, thank God. She doesn't even look like she's regretting it. My spit of potatoes is definitely what she was going for.

"Words of advice; you need to be more careful about getting to another mansion of any of these witnesses, alone, let alone have food served for your appetite only. This is still very much a 'poisonous' time to trust someone, anyone. Each time it has its way proven."

I was too busy focusing on not spilling any crucial information about any of the cases, as Detective Jevon has on many occasions reminded me of, I completely forgot about the possibility that the next killer might make a move again, and that I or any of us could be next.

Everything is going just fine and seemingly upright until we slightly hear the doorbell ring. What surprises me more is the guest on the door who barges into the dining room as if it's perfectly fine and habitual for the landowner sitting just across from me. It's none other than Detective Jevon. He is too at me for the exact same reason.

"What are you doing here, and why do we meet again?" He doesn't say it out loud but I can hear him speaking these exact same words in his mind just by looking at him.

Detective Jevon gives inviting glaring eyes to Miss Decima asking to talk in private, then she follows him while patting my left shoulder softly on the way. Naturally, my instinct tells me to follow them to know what's going on, by the old-fashioned way of eavesdropping through the gap of the door.

I don't usually care that much about other people's business like this, especially when good food is just in front of me; but this one's different. Something about their dynamic that's so peculiarly interesting and intriguing, and for that reason I must know even from the other side of this door.

"Didn't you know 'how' to call?" From what I can hear, Miss Decima starts to light up a cigarette while questioning his manner.

"What I want to talk about is not something to be discussed over the phone, Decima. Do you know how bad this is, for you?"

"No."

Miss Decima replies very calmly in a deeper voice. Sounds to me like she either doesn't know or simply doesn't care at all what's hitting her. Still, how I wish I could see their expressions too as a bonus.

"Do you know how bad this is for me too? For my career if they know I'm even talking to you about this right now?"

"Can you get to the point? Sigh."

And this time, I can even tell that her smoke is blowing straight to his face as he coughs in response.

"Tell me why there was a *crystalline metalloid* purchase on your credit card statement four months ago."

"What is that? Besides, that credit card was stolen around that time. I'm sure you've known that by now if you really are good at what you're doing 'for the people'. Also, I don't think you can just check on my credit card like this. Didn't you need a warrant first?"

"Well, I can, to a suspect! Don't you play games again with me, Decima. How can I know if that's not you making a false report to anticipate getting caught such as on this very day? I know you better than everybody else that you're smarter than this."

"That's probably why we never work, never did, never will."

"Don't tell me that was all because I never trusted you, because I did, and–"

Beep. Beep. Beep.

And? And? Argh, dammit, why now! All of that soap opera is put on hold by the ringing which seems to come from Detective Jevon's phone. I'm just happy that my 'Argh' on immediate reflex is just in my head, not being voiced. Otherwise, I'd be caught guilty for eavesdropping.

"What? When? I'll get there right away."

Then he hangs up.

"What? What's going on?" Miss Decima sounds genuinely worried this time, probably because his face looks much worse after the call. I can't tell for sure due to this door not having any window or enough gap for my eyes to sneak in.

"There's been... another murder," he replies.

"When?"

"Around this afternoon, they believe. They're still processing the scene. I need to go now, we'll talk again later."

I can hear his steps getting towards the door but as I'm almost ready to quietly run away, he suddenly stops his steps as Miss Decima speaks. So I risk it and wait, just a little bit longer.

"You know, I have an alibi for today. Right on the other side of this very door."

OH NO!

Does she know I'm outside? Am I that loud? I thought I was pretty quiet the whole time. Or is she just saying that metaphorically?

"That means she is too, for now, for the both of you," he replies.

As soon as he opens the door, I don't have enough time to stray as far from the door. I mean, what am I supposed to do after all that? If I run, the noise from my pace will narc on me anyway. Both ways will still end up the same, this awkward position.

Miss Decima walks out of the study room afterward and smiles at me as soon as she sees me too. Much the opposite of the detective's gesture towards me.

"Each other's shield, you might say?" Her words to me, with

that big smile on her face, looking as if she feels perfectly safe about anything that is going to happen, no matter how sooner or later.

Curious.

But she definitely knows I've been listening; from her expression, I'm sure. However, she doesn't seem angry or even a little bit furious about it.

"You're not curious at all about who it is, Decima?" He soon walks back in a bit of a slow motion, just to ask that.

Wasn't he supposed to be in a hurry?

"No," Miss Decima responds so calmly, as the increasing insinuation on her voice verifies it straight up. She then exhales the smoke confidently.

"You don't care at all?"

"No," she replies again the exact same way, like a broken record.

"I never care anyway who dies, as long as it's not me," she adds as she blows her beloved ciggy once more, not looking at Detective Jevon.

"But I am! Who is it?" I force myself into the conversation without shame that I sound a bit like a little child full of curiosity.

I do want to know who the victim is. I wonder if it's someone we know. To my surprise, Miss Decima giggles at my peculiarity as she seems to be entertained by it.

"Halihan Dunbar," he says in a rush before proceeding to run.

The victim is much to my surprise, and apparently for Miss Decima too as her cigarette falls unexpectedly. I thought she said she wouldn't care; but anyway, maybe it was just another one of her acts, acting ignorant and cool.

"Could it be...," Miss Decima unconsciously speaks to herself in tremble but apparently much to the unwanted audience in her frame of mind; as when she realises I hear what she says, she acts herself out by bowing down to pick up her cigarette; no longer with her short-displayed empathy, as if she hasn't said a word.

As for me, I urge my legs to run following the detective to go where the new crime scene is. I'll leave the 'Could it be' for later, perhaps much much later.

27

~

Maybe I'm Not So Stupid After All

"You are one snoopy child, aren't you?"

Detective Jevon seems to consider my curious behaviour as one that only children ever possess.

"I'm twenty five years old. I don't know if you can still call that a child," I respond in a more mature voice to force a level playing field.

"I can, if one still acts like one," he smiles this time.

My heart is surprised by his apparent benign but I decide not to say any further. I don't want to wreck that wonderful mood of his; I have the tendency to do that.

Considering how I assume his age is the same or slightly older than Miss Decima, I would place his age somewhere between five and eight years older than me. Regardless, my politeness has come down unfairly by a significant amount.

I'm also still trying to figure out the right time and way to know what really happened between him and the thirty year-old socialite. They seem to come from a totally different world, yet intertwined almost indefinitely. I remember how I thought the world would need to turn upside down first before they could even be together; maybe the world had, in a way. Would be interesting to know how they first met too. It wasn't any clear at all from Miss Decima's cryptic storytelling; for all we both know, it could all be fiction, the stories she told, the narratives I told.

I've seen my late aunt and uncle's mansion, Miss Decima's, and now Sir Halihan's. To entertain myself with a better depiction, the latter is a version of the darkest fairy tale castle I've ever seen. It's like he chose to live in a cataclysmic point in time from the outside world for as long as he lives... lived, sorry. I'm not even sure if the wall's colour is just very dark or it's from the type of the wood. Maybe oak or mahogany or certain species of teak, I'm not sure. Almost no shade of light whatsoever. I start to wonder how he read all of these books lingering on every wall flying off every ceiling of the house, or if they were just for decorations.

We proceed to the entrance of, no big surprise there now, another study room. However, this time the lookout is far different from Uncle Gershom's.

What do I think?

Besides being far darker and with more peculiar woods, it's also more messy than the rest. Open books everywhere with handwritten notes all over the pages. Scattered money on the table in which the wind from the slightly open window isn't strong enough to move the money into the flaming fireplace. Lastly, his face on top of that mountain of green bills with both of his hands still holding some of them as they're tightly wrapped in his knuckles. I would assume that he died while counting his money and decided to stick with them on his last dying breath hoping they would follow him to the afterlife. Though the mess is beyond anyone's reach, it's clear that it has been his own doing and not a break-in attempt; unless someone has seriously given it too much effort attempting to make it look like one.

"What do you think?" The detective surprises me with a question familiar to mine.

As I'm still going around the room looking for something useful , I don't think I currently have anything in mind that can impress him. But I guess staying quiet doesn't help with that either. This time I might even be on the contrary to the old me, that maybe risking saying something wrong may even be less harmful than not saying anything at all.

"Was he possibly poisoned too, with arsenic?" I respond as I smell the same garlic scent when I go near his body.

"I would say so myself. He probably started to choke while counting his money," he replies with his hand on his chin.

"Could it be that the poison was on the money? I mean, he seems to have had that old nasty habit. Judging by all of this money, he probably didn't keep most of his fortune in the bank. Maybe he was licking some to keep count and died in the process?"

"My thoughts are the same. *We*'ll know later for sure after they're being processed."

We? Did he just say 'we'? As in we - me and him? But it could also mean him and the police. Oh well. Forget it. Maybe I was being too hopeful.

"Sir, are we able to move the body now?" One of the police officers raises his question, and as Detective Jevon nods, Sir Halihan is quickly moved into a body bag ready for a transit to the autopsy room.

Right before the closing, something slips out of Sir Halihan's knuckles. To our shock, there's this one odd and crumpled $100 bill with something written on it.

I KILLED CORINA

Who is Corina?

The handwriting seems hurried and similar with those in the opened books too, not to mention the bungee-jumping line down to the last thirteenth letter that also gets us to think that Sir Halihan actually wrote this down himself, while coughing and choking to death. Could this be that all of these murders are related to this Corina?

"Check with Peter if anyone has any leads to the missing suspect, the doctor," Detective Jevon instructs his subordinates. "And see what we can find about this Corina. Any person or news; anything that has to do with the word Corina, check their relevance to these four murders. Tell them to do it fast!" He then insinuates the last word heavily. "I think we're dealing with a serial killer here."

"So you also think Aunt Petunia, Uncle Gershom, and their neighbour's murder - they're all related?" I raise my voice too this time.

"It's hard not to somehow, even though the old lady wasn't among the twelve people on the dining table," he answers me rapidly.

Now I can see that he's not being as secretive as he used to towards me. I'm glad.

At night, we all come back to our own residence with the biggest clue 'Corina'. Strange. I don't think I know anyone with that name. I don't even think I've ever heard the name before. But then again, it could be that I just missed it.

Once again, I somehow don't think Doctor Godric is behind all of this. Like, if it was him, why did he poison himself during the first murder? What for? After such a neat killing, why went reckless for the second one? Why did he run away? Did he know something else? Why should he kill the neighbour? Why killed the godfather? Did he commit one murder but not the others? Was he framed? Or, is there more than one murderer? Did it include him? Or, is the murderer actually among us the other eight witnesses? More like seven - why did I even include myself in the possibility. And why did I even include my parents? It should've been five. Wait, unless...

All of these never-ending thoughts, they urge me to stay awake even when my body says, "Stop it, it's already two a.m!"

I need dull repetitions to think of, to clear my tangled head in the most horrendous way. Most daringly, I honestly really want to catch the killer with my own hands. I mean, who knows who's next or if I'm next? I sincerely hope the devil doesn't touch any of my family. Should I tell my parents to leave town? But would that make them suspicious instead? And it's not like I'm going with them. I want to stay here, even though it'll probably get me killed.

Argh, so many questions and ideas in my head. So hard to get out when I'm already inside this circle of insomnia, all round and about filled with wonders and worries, all alone.

Alone.

Idonia, how is she by the way? She must feel more and more lonely and horrible these days. The murderer; doesn't he or she know what a miserable little child they've made her? I probably should visit her tomorrow, I mean today.

I also wonder; who's her next guardian? It was Uncle Gershom, then Sir Halihan. If there's no more Sir Halihan, would that make my dad the guardian next in line? And that would make her my little sister, wouldn't it?

Actually, what if these unsolved murders have anything to do with the guardianship, maybe about the money Idonia has inherited? Even worse, would the murderer eventually kill the little girl? I hope not.

Sleep.

I need to sleep.

But the more I urge myself to close my mind even further, the more the others try to break in. So I have to come up with something that is usually able to put me back to sleep as quickly as when the water drips out from a leaf after a rainy day. I slept so many times during my school days and it was usually because of those boring lectures and overweight books we had to read.

So I grab a book and get my body lying comfortably on the carpeted floor. I'm still in my room of course, my body is, but where my spirit is going is still a bit unclear.

Then there it is right now, on the covered creek on the floor, just by the corner right on the edge of where the carpet ends. All there is left to do now is to flip it just a bit so I can open the entrance to the other side of my world, hidden from anyone else but me; I jump right in.

It's dark but it's fine. I have the clearest idea of where the lever is, and as soon as these five fingers skydive towards the pivot, my secret sanctum shows up in full bright line.

A library full of memories, as well as my deepest feelings on record each wrapped with distinctive emotions. I'd say that this is pretty much my palace of thoughts and solicitudes. I haven't been here for quite a while.

The amble that draws me to the marshalled mountains of knowledge with the army of thousands of barricades looking more like a volume of books; each seems to only allow myself, the creator it may be, to step one by one on every stint interval they accordingly sow. The seeds are immediately growing voluntarily. With the length seems endless, the bookshelves humble themselves to just the size of my arms raised. They then spread their wings to perpetuity, rather than sprouting to the nowhere sky that has no day and no night. Their interior is ancient hardcovers of various rustic colours. They can almost be identified just by the golden-dusted initials in voluptuous font right on each side.

I always wonder how to enter it anywhere and anytime I want, but they seem to know better when. They only show themselves when I desperately need them or whenever I think I'm as stupid as a brick that I'm going to fail miserably, such as during exam period, and maybe on the verge of a close death. My deepest secret; I'm giving it enough time to finish my soliloquy without the thought of being wrong, then I survive to reach the conclusion. It's always been more effective this way than when I'm awake.

The round table hovering to the centre with proud gesticulation is not to be underestimated for it has availed itself of leading duty and governance no less to its maximum magical potential. It then asks me with its deep and thunder-bearing voice, "It has been a while, Miss Daedalia. I was wondering when you would ever be coming back."

I was instead wondering when it would ever show up; but it indeed has been the longest time.

And then I realise; that I go, I see, I find, and I gather, always; but I never assemble. Everything is going places like the scattered stars in the galaxy, just waiting for someone, somewhere, anybody to draw the line by connecting the dots that gives them shape and title they do or do not need, similarly to mine as it's still a pure confusion whether I'm as necessary or whether then was the right time to start.

Except now, I will draw the line right here onward and start the mind map.

"Table, do take the stage. We start right now," I say to the four legs of wonder, and nods he is to me. I talk a bit differently and position myself as the king, or queen, in this place; vigorous, kind, never confused, never again backing down.

This particular table always does its job more than it's supposed to, as it's almost like it's having this telepathic strain to my thoughts and delineates on its head the abridgement perfectly, while convening the rest of the details on its body without even seconds of delay. On top of that, classical music is playing vociferously across the space, as it should. Once in a while, it adds a restless deejay beat according to the beat of my heart when I'm getting close to something.

28

~

Library Full of Memories

Day Minus Three Months, about ninety days before Aunt Petunia's death; the apparent murder of Wilbert Cruikshank, my uncle and aunt's gardener before he went dead, before my uncle and aunt went dead.

What more do I know about him?

Soon after, one of the magical bookshelves understands my exigency for information and flies one of its books out to me. Then, so quickly the khaki-coloured book hops onto my palm. It really hops, like a rabbit, and I find it very cute. I think the book is sort of smiling at me too. I bow my head facing the shelf showing my respect, grasping in the royalty vibe too deep in here. The bookshelf makes an effort to bow back. The funny thing is, as it bows, all the books inside are sliding away. They're squeaking like mice on the run, but none of them are falling off.

What I anticipate from this book is something I've seen that I forgot about this old man, something I won't be aware of in my awakened state. It comforts me how they're still stored safely down here.

There it is, on the first page. A headline from a news article I must have seen before. Did I read it through carefully or skim it? I'll know once I turn the page.

Not much in here. Wilbert Cruikshank, seventy nine years of age, died of natural causes. No mention of possible foul play either. Some of the letters are blurred, most likely because I did skim read it as it only stores what I really read, but there wasn't that much to begin with. The headline also seems so small, it looks like the kind that no one really cares about. Since an autopsy wasn't even performed, that was pretty much it; that's all I've got about his death.

Then Day One, Aunt Petunia's death. I set it as where on the line the series might all begin from here. Just as if a lightning rod from my thoughts is bent over onto the table, it replays in a fast mode, then slow, then fast again all the memories so vividly onto the enigmatic screen on top. I think the speed is highly dependent on my current sieve attitude and disposition, as my mind unconsciously tries to discern between what seems to be important and what's not. My hands grasp hard on the table too, firm and solid as my eyes try to connect soulfully with the visual catching my full and foremost attention. All of the sudden, the table fasts forward to my mom's interview; and the words 'three months' are repeated over and over and over again.

Three months. Isn't that around the same time as to when the gardener died? That can't just be a coincidence, can it? Thereafter, a line appears in the sky across my head, continuing to move itself almost like connected dotted stars but with numbers and names of significance, forming a timeline. Does this mean there really is a connection between Aunt Petunia's murder and that poor old man they all deemed to be trivial?

Say, perhaps Doctor Godric is really the culprit that did this to Aunt Petunia. But if that was so, why did he have to put poison on his glass too? To remove himself as a suspect? And why didn't he die too? I guess just a smaller dose of arsenic kept him alive, but how come it killed Aunt Petunia at once?

Unless, Aunt Petunia had already been poisoned within that three-month interval, little by little. Her symptoms, as the screen now shows me running into her, the last three months she was still alive. Rapid heartbeat, rather quick and shallow breathing, tiredness and confusion - I'm quite sure now. That novel says the same thing too. In that case, only a small amount was necessary to kill her that night, in accumulation. But why gradually? To make her suffer or there're some other reasons? And how did Aunt Petunia take the poison for a prolonged time and never even noticed?

These branches of possibilities are making me confused that I'm no longer standing up. Luckily, a sofa nearby manages to race itself to where I'm going to plunge. Afterward, my right palm clutches my forehead to contain my dispersed thoughts. Much better.

As I sit down nicely, one of the books - a really big one -

comes up to me. Its gentleness softs my emotion as it's bringing me a cup of chamomile.

Chamomile, of course.

Day Ten, Uncle Gershom's tragic death in his very early fifties. Seeing my dad being dazed from time to time from missing his brother, it gives me the stimulus for a sweet revenge. Stopping this inhuman serial killer before *it* murders again, like a trapper catching a wild animal, whose madness has been disturbing our peace.

The knife was already missing before he even came into the room. I don't think that it was possible for Doctor Godric to take the knife beforehand. Uncle Gershom was the only one with the key to the study room. As I know how much he looked up to my father, he was following his steps in only giving the key to the butler when it needed cleaning.

The butler, Mr. Catullus; could it be? But what was even his motivation? Were my uncle and aunt treating him poorly out of our imagination? I'm missing something again from this, just like the missing bell.

Oh yes, the bell.

It was missing from the crime scene. But why was it missing? Unless, someone else rang it as part of the plan.

The killer. Yes, it must be the real killer's doing.

The bell was not even in the room when it all happened.

Because, how could it be? We were there the minute the bell rang and Mr. Catullus came straight away before us. Maybe, the culprit killed Uncle Gershom, then went outside and rang the bell. But Doctor Godric was there. Could he have seen or glimpsed at the murderer? But if he had done so, he wouldn't have run away, as it was all happening so fast. But that means, the killer wouldn't even have the time to hide the bell. The killer would have to pretend to come to the premise to show up to form an alibi, then leave to throw away the bell somehow.

You know what's crazy? Detective Jevon's perfect timing fits this theory like a dream, but not the chamomile; whereas Mr. Catullus with the chamomile but not the bell. Argh!

Day Eleven. The murder of Miss Edda Burwood is one that I've not had full confirmation of its relevance as she wasn't among the twelve people in the dining room that night Aunt Petunia died, and yet I have this brawny tingling feeling in my bones that it still is connected. But then again, what was even the connection?

From what Bou has told me, based on her conversation with that poor old woman's nurse, Avila, the seventy three year-old victim was never married. She did have depression, but it's not like the killer was doing any justice by killing her. That's just sick.

So was her reason for depression the reason why she was killed instead? I hope it's not because she's never tied the knot.

Oh! The rope!

I remember the weird smell. It appears again now as fumes in the colour of hazel right before my eyes. Why does my brain want it to be the colour of such, I wonder. Such a familiar warm and sweet amber aroma being a forced accomplice to such a murderous object that had no intention to be so. Where have I smelled this before? I'm pretty sure I have. The screen shows me so many possibilities that I lose track of which one matters. And let's be honest, I don't think the memory of me smelling an essential oil bottle in a random store will help solve the puzzle.

Day twelve, the latest of the case. The murder of Sir Halihan Dunbar, who was just a year short from his fortieth birthday. That also makes him about eleven years younger than both Uncle Gershom and Aunt Petunia.

One thing I'm most curious about.

'I Killed Corina'.

By all means, do I even know anything about this ever-mentioned Corina? Cleverly, the table knows what to do and shows me on the screen anything I ever unconsciously store, any memories with 'Corina' in it. It's almost like a news feed that I can scroll. Some of the headlines are blurry too, with the only word clear is 'Corina' on them, so I still have no idea if any of them is relevant.

One thing has caught my attention though.

'*Corina Bailhache pleaded guilty to a series of murders. Sadly, it does not stop there.*'

Thirteen years ago.

But then the rest is again, blurred.

Can this be a coincidence?

In that instance too, my vision is brought back to the reality here and now, as both of my eyes are unfolded by a touch of an early morning air from the small gap the window has allowed. I'm also still lying on the floor. Therefore, in view of having woken up from my reverie once more to summon my knowledge, the first thing that passes by my languorous mind is to forage on any articles about 'Corina Bailhache'. Really, the last name is the only additional information I need.

29

~

A Long Forgotten Piece of Puzzle

Victoria Daily News

CORINA BAILHACHE
PLEADED GUILTY
TO A SERIES OF MURDERS
SADLY IT DOES NOT STOP THERE ...

Nine known dead, two attempted;
one might still be alive

VICTORIA, Dec. 11. - 'I didn't do it' turned into a full confession of 'I did everything' just less than a year later, as

inscribed carefully by the lead prosecutor's winning announcement post trial.

"We have been burdened heavily by the incredible amount
of puzzled traces in the past, but we are finally able to put all
the pieces back together. Justice has ultimately been served today, as also fully desired by the family with the broken hearts,
the second the juries have agreed to find the defendant *guilty as
charged*," said Webley Wexler, Chief State Prosecutor of Victoria, one of the most populated states in the country.

The court was filled in majority with audience pleased by
the ruling, but not at all from the defendant's loyal side that
solemnly argued that the result was heartless - in total incon-
sideration of the pregnancy maturity of the defendant, despite
the cold-blooded killings the millionaire heiress had successfully
committed to her dear surroundings seemingly so effortlessly.
Further the blow, the plea for her transfer to the mental health
institution has also been rejected, in which its probity has also
been concluded by her final crooked-smile to the court that gave
everyone who saw, cold shivers and fiddly goosebumps.

CHRONOLOGY OF MURDERS

"The first one was pretty much random, just to know what
it felt like in real life," the lady with the red hair confessed with a
remorseless smile as she was let to take the stand by her defence
team, supposedly to defend herself. Her sky-fees team of lawyers
were seen smacking their forehead, showing their receival of an
incontestable loss.

The victim, Lessica Poore, was one of the young house-maids in her residence when she was drugged to death in her sleep. "It was ineffable, a feeling I had concealed for so long," she continued with a proud sigh and laugh. Just like that, she had established her first killing at the age of twenty two, with a prominent indication of a conspicuous psychopath.

The second and third murder, no later than five years apart from the first, is her late mother's companion, Haidee Agnelli, the unlucky attendee of the annual Bailhache party. She was one of the two carefully chosen to slurp on the wine that had been tampered with arsenic traces; then her biological father, Lambert Bailhache.

"A first class betrayal," she strongly mentioned in court, as the already-married woman was evidently implied to have an illicit affair with no other than her own father before the tragic death of Gretchen Williams, Corina's biological mother, due to natural causes.

It was within that half a decade she was away, as it had been stoutly emphasised by the prosecutor, that she had been putting together scenarios in her head to fulfil her grudge out of boredom, eventually realising her murderous plans not far from home. If only her home was nowhere to be found.

Just less than a week later, the second victim's husband, Rayner Williams, was found dead right after the burial cere-mony of her adulterous wife; this time with a dagger impaled right on his forehead. Her own housemaids finally confirmed the truth, that Corina had purchased the peculiar dagger long ago during her study days abroad and brought it back home upon her return. That was why it took quite a while to have it tracked down.

When being asked for a reason, she simply answered, "He looked so sad instead of being happy that his cheating wife was gone, so I thought he probably wanted to go to where she went too," this time she didn't smile. "I probably wouldn't have done it if he hadn't been so *sad*," she added whilst insinuating the last part on purpose, as if it was all her victim's fault and not hers. Her what-a-shame contour shaped the court room's unbelief even further.

The fifth murder happened just one day after the fourth, when a long-known depressed old woman, Mirabai Dellaforte, was found dead just a few blocks from where Corina lived. "She drugged the poor old woman with the same poison of less lethal dose, and hung her to her death, just out of curiosity," Detective Scrabble Morrisson further described the murder was heinous and a complete misdemeanour, even for someone the felon had barely even known - mere stranger.

The next day, the sixth murder was finalised when Corina successfully put traces of arsenic in a bunch of money accurately forecasted out of knowledge to fall in the hands of Galen Hall upon his love for counting them by hands. Galen was a young fellow of exactly Corina's age and perceived by his peers as an old-money-wannabe, who also happened to be Corina's own *quondam beau* during her study. The murder might be the first of many that she had long started predicating, the moment the man was found cheating on her with both a shockingly male prostitute and a younger female colleague named Bathsheba

Shand. Corina on the court was seen to have no hard feelings whatsoever with his seemingly same-sex interest affair as she had many times expected; but it was the latter that really set her rancour on fire, as she was vividly reminded again by her father's betrayal.

The seventh murder, just the next day after the previous, with a well-known wayward victim only at the age of thirteen, was last seen to be with Corina on the day of her murder. Ludmila Simpkin's body was found sleeping breathlessly in the cold dark air of the midwinter solstice not far from where the garden in the orphanage she lived in was. The cancer stick was *generously* given by none other than Corina with ulterior motives.

"If only the fact was known from the start, her arrest would have happened a lot sooner," Detective Scrabble Morrisson regretted the secrecy behind the institution.

The next murder, the eighth, which also happened on the very next day, was when the clues leading to Corina's felonious acts finally started to illuminate. She had been working on getting her firearm licence with the same murderous intention, presumably out of boredom, quite contrasting the *crystalline metalloid* way she had committed many times before; but her urge for murder managed to exceed her patience that she decided to get a silencer and go to the house of her late ex-boyfriend's former love, Bathsheba Shand, and fired the weapon right to her chest.

"That fake woman got what she deserved. Sending me that bull 'how are you' crap right after that stupid Galen broke up with me. She thought she'd won, but that bullet hole showed who the real winner was. I've never been happier," Corina admitted with no shame, and claimed to be the 'hero of the brokenhearted' in front of everyone in the court.

Ironically, that same bullet on the victim's torso was eventually what got Corina connected to the murder in the first place. Her exotic blue car was also seen parked right in front of the victim's house, the night of the murder.

The next murder was committed afterward, a week after the precursory. Godiva Weaver, who Corina has described as an untalented vain. The victim was someone even all of her extended family members couldn't stand, she further claimed. The former background singer, whose body was found floating in the shallow of vomited blood in her apartment bathtub a few days later, was engaged to one of her cousins, much to his family's brawny disapproval; and while the delay was caused by her cautiousness towards Bathsheba Shand's murder investigation at the time, she ultimately decided to go on with the kill as she wanted it to be one of the good deed murders she perceived she could have performed for the last time before she got arrested. She was correct about the arrest.

FATAL FATE POST-TRIAL

During the approximately nine months from Corina's long overdue detainment to the final hearing, it was obvious that her bump was getting bigger and bigger; however, the paternal origin to the baby in her belly was kept a secret. The heartless lady with a heart-beating human being in her stomach has been inordinately proud to her bone when speaking in detail about what she discerned as her lifetime achievements - the murders - regardless of what her notable lawyers have silently cried-screaming not to do. Nevertheless, never a word from her mouth about the man in her life that is deemed responsible for the foetus.

Being an only child, Corina has always been the sole inheritor of the Bailhache's millions of dollar estate; but things turned into a staggering change when just a couple of hours after her last spine-chilling smile was seen to leave the court awaiting for her death penalty date, her water broke. This leads to uncertainty of whether they, one of them, or none, will survive.

"We are making sure that the hospital is doing everything they can to save them, and our team is still on the clock to do everything we can to take care of the rest in Miss Corina Bailhache's best interest," Halihan Dunbar, one of the defence lawyers gave his comment in a hurry when being asked about the ongoing operation.

"We have successfully got justice served the way we see fit, which has not been easy; the ruling, the victims' families are pleased to hear about the death penalty. It is now up to God to decide," Webley Wexler concluded his point of view, and so are we.

Victoria TV Tube
Time Capsule D|-13Y0M|

BREAKING NEWS HEADLINES

(11/12 11:59 PM) SERIAL KILLER CORINA BAIL-HACHE IS DEAD, BUT HER BABY SURVIVES |View|

(12/12 6:13 AM) FATE OF SERIAL KILLER'S BABY REMAINS A SECRET |View|

(12/12 9:24 AM) LAWYERS GIVE NO COMMENT ON SERIAL KILLER'S BABY AND ESTATE |View|

(13/12 3:40 PM) SERIAL KILLER'S BABY IS FEMALE AND MISSING |View|

(16/12 2:22 PM) SERIAL KILLER'S FAMILY FORTUNE FALLS TO BABY, BUT BABY IS STILL MISSING |View|

30

~

A Fatal Demerit Long Overdue

My ocean blue sedan arrives very early in the morning at the police station, but I don't immediately step out of it. Everything is just too much at the moment. They all keep spinning around in my brain without order. I guess I finally understand now what it feels like to really have it all that makes up too much information of relevance and riddles.

But those news about Corina Bailhache, they're just unbelievably ridiculously shocking to me. Makes me wonder if the news journalist had shifted track into novel writing instead; he or she sounded so immersed in the story. They're like nine series of jaw-dropping dramas. The characters are just seriously disturbed, especially the main one. I almost can't believe that those happened but no one seems to remember. So many about it I can't even make any sense of; why has no one ever brought this up and why hasn't the police even found this yet? Even Sir Halihan's name is there! I know they happened a long time ago and so far away from here, and here's just a mere small town, but all these murders could have probably been avoided if someone had just come forward!

The vibe of the story is almost like the fall of a great psycho heiress whose psychology as a serial killer I can't comprehend. She's like this eerie glow in the night sky; misunderstood, unappreciated, dangerous when it rains. No one seems to love her, or maybe she just doesn't understand the meaning of love, even when she has everything. She seems smart but naive; caring but it also sounds like she's just fond of killing people. Was she born like that or was she just nurtured that way? As I was reading the article, I kept thinking; how in the hell is this not a fiction?

Eventually, what dominates inwardly within the mind starts to transmute physically into a form of migraine. I shift my mind astray a little while; it helps tune the pain down. I smirk occasionally because I think I know now the reason why Madame Hilda thinks negatively about me, the trifling resemblance I can't help but notice. But doesn't that mean she already knew about the case? Why didn't she clearly tell the police then? Just like that, the migraine comes back.

I really need to get my thoughts organised, like sorting them out from the beginning and putting them back nicely in order. This gradual peace begins to escort me to a relief from the slow torment of thumping hemicrania. I am no God, I don't know everything; but my brain keeps inappropriately trying to make it as the One, until it realises its somatic limitation.

So here it goes, now or never, both of my feet get out of the sleeping vehicle in slow motion.

"Is Detective Jevon here?"

He's probably half mutant, one that can hear from miles afar; because by the time I finish speaking the last word, he's already here. I'm glad that he's actually not as hyperborean as he used to be to me anymore, as he welcomes me to sit on one of these uncomfortable dull-looking chairs in this isolated room. My first time here. I'm excited of course; but how come as soon as my back engages the spine of the chair, I feel like one of those criminals? Nevermind.

"Wilbert who?" He raises his eyebrows so noticeably as I keep on explaining my findings. His right brow looks like it's diving to the other side.

From his voice thereafter, it's apparent to me that he has underestimated the cause of this poor old man's death, just like the rest of this institution. There isn't even a single trace of him anywhere here. Weird.

"By the way, the old woman's toxic report came back. Positive for arsenic; and, you would not believe this - paper trace."

"Paper?"

"Burnt," he says, "And not just her, but in the dead lawyer's case as well," he continues perplexedly, sending us both in quandary.

What is going on? Paper? I didn't know they could do that. Talking from the perspective of someone who had tasted a bit of a newspaper article in her mouth when she was very little - I just wanted to know what paper tasted like.

"And your aunt's toxic report came back too," he added with a hefty nod.

He doesn't finish the sentence but he knows his expression will finish the rest; so do I.

"Ahem, 'Madame cannot sleep without a cup of chamomile tea every night', one of the maids told me this."

"So you think that's when she started to be slowly poisoned?"

"It's a good habit, isn't it? I think that makes it a good avenue for the culprit to do what he did... or she... I don't know."

"Makes sense. Well, the toxic report does say that it might have been going on for about three months or so."

"Three months?"

"Yes. Why? It's just an estimate though."

"That's when Wilbert Cruikshank died!"

After that, a tranquil surmise follows.

"So you still think it's related?"

"I just feel I've been hearing 'three months' too many times, maybe that's part of the why too," and to this response of mine he laughs.

"You know, you might actually make a good detective."

"I am? Really?"

"You think you'd be interested?"

Second tranquil surmise repeats, dominated by me.

"I don't know, I don't think I can. Do I want to? I don't know, I don't know," my insecurity gets the best of me again.

"Really? I thought you'd be more interested than that. Surely your behaviour hasn't been saying the same thing."

Actually, I thought so too; but as always, I choose to hide what I really want behind what I think I'm capable of doing - nothing.

"By the way, ahem," I cough just a bit later hoping it'll get rid of my blushing, "Did you... did you find the bell in my uncle's murder case?"

"Oh yes, I was getting there. No actually, which has got me thinking too. Maybe the killer still has it?"

So it really is missing. Weird.

"Maybe that missing doctor still has it," he continues.

"So, you still think he's the murderer?"

"Honestly, who knows at this point. This has all been a string of conundrum serial arsenic cases."

"Yes, conundrum indeed. So, all the cases have arsenic traces?"

"Can you imagine? Even traces were found on the dagger!" He almost screams. "And lots of them on the money in the lawyer's murder case."

"Oh!" I suddenly remember why I'm coming here in the first place.

"Speaking of serial arsenic cases," I proceed hysterically, "Do you know about this case?"

As I show him the news article I read this morning, his eyes squint to the unwitting and his full expression gradually reaches a disbelief; even his body nerves are struggling to comprehend.

"It's just very oddly similar. And the Simpkin, Sir Halihan; they're all there!"

I continue with a little bit of proud feeling and a pinch of vain underestimation towards him that I immediately regret thereafter. I found it the hard way, no good ever comes from being all that.

With a stampeding heart too, I slowly encourage, "I think we should go to Miss Dec–"

Suddenly, Detective Jevon cuts me short and immediately gets both of his feet on the floor up straight with an explosion noise from his shoes. He didn't let me finish my sentence.

"We need to go now, to where that little girl is!" Whilst he is all into his trepidation, he doesn't forget to send more troops to find the missing suspect.

Corina Bailhache's seventh victim, Ludmila Simpkin.

'Simpkin', same surname as Doctor Godric Simpkin. He must have noticed that immediately too, for he asks the rest to research all about her to establish the missing suspect's motive. Naturally, I'm just shadowing wherever he goes, and no one seems to be brave enough to stop me now. Not even Peter, who's just looking at me with great disorder. With all this process, I wonder if perhaps my deduction is wrong after all.

"You should have told me this earlier, the first time you got your eyes on this," he says with a hint of disappointment that I don't fully understand.

Maybe he should blame the others for not doing more proper research - my annoyed mood takes over all my feelings.

We're running to where our car is. Mine apparently is parked just next to his without me even realising. Talk about fluke.

As he bows down against the long window of his car, he mumbles, "Enough is enough. We need to stop this madness."

He seemingly talks to himself, until he glimpses at me before the sight of him from my view disappears.

"We're on our way to the mansion," he instructs without being really clear, but I think I get what he means.

Yes, it must be that mansion, again.

I still can't believe that they still let Idonia stay here, even after all those heinous crimes inside and surrounds it. I'm told that Idonia is unbelievably persistent to stay, and that she has used the supremacy of commiseration against the mighty dictum; the brave little kid I didn't expect. That peculiar room of hers seems to be her shelter after all, so I guess she only feels safe here, her forever familiar place.

Upon arrival, we can see that Mrs. Oriel and some of the servants are already waiting at the gate. I think Detective Jevon made a call on the way here so they were already expecting us, I mean him.

As Sir Halihan is no longer alive, I guess she's now in charge of Idonia. Perhaps she's the next godmother in line? I don't think it was mentioned before, but I might have just missed it.

"I really hope this is not true. What kind of monster is going to murder a little child?" Mrs. Oriel screams with an extremely bright pale face as the sun kisses her skin; at least her *act* shows she's really worried about Idonia.

"Where is Idonia?" Detective Jevon asks while rushing in like the rest of us.

"Inside the library, with a governess," Mrs. Oriel responds.

Arriving there, we both see Idonia and Miss Gretchen, the governess, looking at us with absolute incertitude as to what is going on.

"Thank heavens it's not too late," Detective Jevon looks brighter than the current sunshine outside, seeing Idonia's completely breathing and alive.

Feeling more relaxed, he takes the time to sit next to the confused little girl and asks the governess to go outside to talk alone with the kid whose mind he has made jumbled. My steps are naturally following where the governess goes, out the door, convincing myself to act with more respectful manners this time; but surprisingly Detective Jevon wants me to stay in the room too.

He trusts me more with the case now. I'm smiling.

"How are you feeling?"

This is how he starts the conversation.

He then asks her if she ever heard Aunt Petunia and Uncle Gershom talking about 'some things' where in response she asks back what he means by 'some things'.

"Unforgettable things," he answers.

But to our surprise, she looks at me as a way to respond. I don't know what to say, so I just smile at her and hold her hands. That's when she closes both her eyes just to open them up again a short few seconds later. Her eyes are projecting fire, later revealing the following.

"Daughter of a murderer," she says, "and you're everything she was," she adds after a thorough silence. "That is the last thing *he* said to me," she ends it with a gesture of dauntlessness, unmoved.

She must be talking about Uncle Gershom.

"Anything else?" Detective Jevon never looks more concerned.

Beep. Beep. Beep.

Detective Jevon's cell phone suddenly rings. My eyes can sneak a peek that it's Miss Decima who's calling. He's making a late effort to hide his phone, then flicks the screen with just a tiny movement and shifts his focus back on Idonia.

"Corina," she sounds rather hesitant this time.

"But I still don't know what to do after–"

Beep. Beep. Beep.
Another one.

Detective Jevon cuts the sentence short by shifting his eyes back to the screen then back again to Idonia.

"How about any arguments? Maybe Doctor Godric came by once and made a scene around here?"

"I don't know, maybe–"

Beep. Beep. Beep.
Again.

And he's still ignoring her call.

"Alright, how about your biological mother, was it–"
"That is all I know I'm afraid... her name, her... no more. No face, no photograph I can relate to... none. So if you please, I have more studies to do," she cuts back Detective Jevon's corroboration words in return.

She stares at him quickly and annoyed. She doesn't like the rush the detective imposes her on, though I don't think I can blame him. Detective Jevon is just very keen on closing these cases as soon as possible, for his sanity sake. He ignores Miss Decima's calls after all, for the physical conversation.

While Detective Jevon decides to continue interviewing the others which he thinks are more informative, I choose to stay by Idonia's side. Mrs. Oriel is her guardian now but I'm curious about how she really treats her. Hopefully she'll be honest with me.

"I don't know, fake as usual," she answers, but her innocent smirk lets me know that she knows I've realised it too.

"She insisted on being my guardian and fought with Mrs. Lesley for that. No one, not even her, ever cared enough about me before. What a fake," she adds.

Wow, even this thirteen year-old girl can perceive the concealed truth. But what surprises me more is the tone of her voice this time. She almost sounds like Miss Decima there.

I don't really know what else it is to say; but as if she's aware of my blankness, she asks me with her watery innocent eyes, "Do you think I am everything my mother was?"

"Of course not!" I immediately howl.

Her turnaway head suggests to me that she thinks my answer is either a lie or good enough of an answer.

I stay for another ten minutes with her until Detective Jevon suddenly barges in, surprising us so unexpectedly. Even Miss Gretchen who seems to have been snooping almost falls to the side of her heels involuntarily.

Does he come for me? What for though?

Another murder? Another arsenic case?

Detective Jevon's face looks terribly full with trepidation but tries his best to appear calmer. He's not doing a great job at it; he looks like he's dying.

"It's Decima. She... she... she...," he whispers. His lips are bound speechless ever since, but I already understand everything perfectly.

It can't be.

31

~

Empathy or Curiosity

As soon as our feet force themselves to run, we silently race to our car. Just as we reach the end of the intersection, we're stopped by a familiar light of vermillion, slowing us down so soon. As soon as the green light is back in charge, I step on my pedal hard and continue on speeding. So does Detective Jevon. Whoever policemen are trying to stop us, they're the ones that are going to be in trouble instead.

Left to the hospital and right is to Miss Decima's mansion. Detective Jevon's car is going to the left based on the blinking light he's just turned on. Mine, it might.

The number on the traffic light still counts down from eight, and by the same amount of flashing of those seconds too, my ego is suddenly plugging out each petal of the illusory stop sign under the sun correspondingly between the two directions.

Eight for left, seven for right, six left and five right, four left, three, two, one.

My car is drifting to the right side of the street, defying all one-way rules and crossing lines to my reckless selfishness for my safety and the others'. I no longer lean towards empathy; don't I want to know how Miss Decima is, and if she survives?

All of us are in the same neighbourhood so it doesn't take that long to reach Miss Decima's grand house. The maid lets me in easily due to my familiar face. She leads me to the dining room where everything is said to be left just the way it was when it happened, where it all went down.

"Where are the police?" I ask.

"They're on their way, I was told. It all happened so quickly, Miss. We called the ambulance first. Oh Miss, what has just happened?" Says Katherine while blowing her nose with a paper towel.

Despite the arrogance I perceive Miss Decima has manifested across the world, everyone here actually really cares about her - all filled with worries and doubts.

"Tell me what happened," I wish them to as we're waiting for the officers.

Everything was going as per usual. Yoga breakfast - whatever that means, morning shower, skincare routine, then usual garden walking with her timely cigarettes. Smoke followed her exorbitantly and everything was just basically her on centre stage with her humble servants unaware of any change in yesterday's script to her ever-switching moods. By the book, everything she does usually depends on what she fits that very second. More than often, they could be unpredictable.

"When exactly did it happen?" I raise more queries.

The clock was set to three and she began her very late lunch with her wondrous chilling around the mansion garden alone with, of course, one cigarette. After half an hour done with her speck of mushroom risotto, she blew another cigarette while walking out quite far from the dining room. That was around the same time she started to have a shorter breath and consequently thump on her chest. Arriving here, she fell down eventually and the rest of the house started to panic. As they were calling the ambulance, she was multitasking between fighting for her life and calling Detective Jevon.

I was there; that must be exactly when it all happened - when we were talking to Idonia.

Hang on.

So, would it be the lunch or the cigarettes that caused her to fall to seizure?

"Who cooked the food today?"

"It was me, Miss. Did she, do you think...," says Catherine with tears this time, thanks to my question.

"Oh no no, we just... we don't know yet, you know. I'm just curious. Where's the cigarette by the way?"

"It's still here, Miss, on the floor. Oh, we almost forgot about this."

Soon after, fortunately, the investigators arrive and collect everything including the dish Miss Decima last ate and the cigarette she last inhaled.

Miss Decima.

Now my body urges to check up on her rather than what alternates the wicked, as if the brain has had its prioritised dam filled. I go back to my car and quickly head on to the hospital. Arriving, I can't seem to find anyone anywhere; not because it's empty, but rather the opposite.

Maybe I should call Detective Jevon, assuming he doesn't hold any grudge on my ignorance and brief runaway, but then I remember that I don't actually have his number. I've never even asked and I always forgot to ask.

"Where have you been?" Detective Jevon suddenly surprised me from behind.

I find the timing of his appearance to be constantly fitting. But he's not looking relieved. Could it be...

"Follow me," he continues.

I haven't even said anything yet.

I follow his steps that lead to a closed door. He keeps on being silent on the way. His right hand presses on the door and pauses temporarily with his head bow down just a pinch, but then he gains back all the strength to push it slowly and let me peek just a little at the strong-willed female patient on the other side of the door, laying in despair.

"She's going to be okay. She's fortunate enough to be alive," he says slowly.

He quickly absorbs his sniffs like he's about to cry but he's going to do whatever it takes not to.

"That's a relief. What about the... credit card charges? The *crystalline metalloid*," I respond.

He seems very surprised, then not. After that, it's my turn to be surprised because I realise he knows I could only get this piece of information by eavesdropping the other night.

"I'm going to call for backups, to keep an eye on her, just in case," he swifts the topic.

"Wait, so at the moment, excluding the doctors, we're the only ones who know she's alive?" My cloud catches the lamp.

"Your point?" He responds.

"What do you think the killer will do? If the killer knows Miss Decima is alive. Will he try to kill her again or proceed anyway to the next?"

"I'm just curious," I add.

He glances at Miss Decima for a while, repeatedly with his lips twisted like he cannot contain that he's thinking very hard right now, but he then steadily closes the door and looks at me again.

"And no one knows she's been poisoned besides us and her maids," he builds up on my argument.

"And the killer," I add.

He calls his department immediately to let them know of the idea to keep it a secret, insistently, then runs to the medical officers to do just the same. Meanwhile, I run to Miss Decima's mansion to also tell them the decree.

What will happen next is what worries me the most.

Considering all of Corina's murders, I have a strong feeling that another heinous crime involving a gun will happen tomorrow. I should call Detective Jevon. Oh wait. Damn. I forgot to ask for his number again, and so I have to retrace my earlier steps of going to the police station, again.

Just as soon as my car parks near the precinct, Detective Jevon's black car is too. We headed off then arrived right at the same time. This fluke of hopefully good coincidence.

I run to where he's about to open the door as fast as my leftover stamina can. I surprise him with a reminder of the news article I've shown him. Turns out, the reason he gets back to the headquarters so early is exactly the same.

Together, we go back inside; along with two other local sherlocks, Detective Potsy Whitlock and Detective Gervase Pierce. They've been helping Detective Jevon without my notice. To my surprise, Detective Jevon has been telling them all about me - my weirdness and my seemingly-sharpness in regards to all the cases; by hook or by crook, I've impressed them too. Ironically, I haven't really impressed myself.

"So, who is it, do you think, Miss?" Detective Gervase seems keen to challenge my deduction as opposed to theirs.

I can feel it in my bones, I can't seem to stop thinking that the key is startlingly obvious - 'fake'.

32

～

Boujee in White

Cigarette

Detective Jevon hands over the odd piece of paper to me. It was crafted in this beautiful handwriting style, as what we all agree on, except in regards to the 'who'.

A cigarette? Is it about... Miss Decima?

"Someone dropped this piece of paper at the station right when Decima was poisoned," he explains.

Curious as traces of arsenic have been confirmed to be found in the last cigarette travelled to Miss Decima's lips. More curious that somehow this handwriting seems familiar to me. It's like I've seen this somewhere before but I can't get around it at the moment.

As the frustration takes control over me, I unconsciously

answer the question Detective Potsy randomly puts up in the air vocally, about who could be the next fly fluttering unknowingly around the spiderweb.

"Oriel Walmsley," I've realised I've just spoken without my awareness being the precedent, again, out loud.

It's like I have no control over my mouth now. I realise that it's all too late for me to back down. What is wrong with me these days? I used to have a brawny brake behind my voice, that it knew best to stay hidden. Now, it just doesn't listen to my tender atelophobia.

Detective Potsy raises his eyebrows. Later I point to that same article again.

"Care to explain to me why she is seen as 'fake'?" Detective Gervase continues his partner's curiosity.

I explain to the three men my view, a perspective which seemingly can only truly come from those within her social circle, and heavily influenced by Miss Decima's outlook. Why, though, I don't feel pleasant at all anymore in the volunteer deliberation of judging her as one anyway?

I want to have this core belief in my heart that every single human on this earth is born good; no monster, no devil, but just innocent to his or her surroundings from their own timid observation, which eventually grows stronger across time and to which direction solely depends on their crossing chosen paths no matter prevailingly right or wrong, and that leads them to go either way, good or bad.

Not excluding Mrs. Oriel's perceived double faces, which Miss Decima has multiple times implied. I'm sure that there's some sort of explanation following her behaviour and leading to this 'fake' accusation as even Idonia has recently precisely justified.

"Are you okay?" Detective Jevon suddenly wakes me up from my own discussion with my thoughts.

"What?" I respond in reflection of my own hallucinatory figure in his eyes; I do seem perplexed.

"You seem to be spacing out," he replies.

My mouth is too careful this time that I lose track flying in my own cloud. The backbone of each of these certified justice premiers are unshakenly shaping bridges with their long arms held steady onto the overpass. On the other hand, I can't seem to even find a safe harbour from the strong storm of my own contemplation. This too shall pass as we continue on what really matters. We believe we don't have a lot of time.

For safety reasons, they decide not to take any risk and send troops to protect not just one or two, but the rest of us. My mom, my dad, myself, Miss Decima, Mrs. Oriel, Mrs. Lesley, Madame Hilda, and Idonia. We are they've got left from the rest of us.

"We need to take every precaution until the killer, or that missing suspect, is found," Detective Jevon is determined.

Doctor Godric is sure one hell of a runner.

I rest my head on the pillow just heavily to the right, hoping that the silk on the cover touches my cheek just nicely.

Where is he? I wonder.

If I were him, what would I be doing right at this very second? Where would I go?

"Where do you think?" Doctor Godric suddenly surprises me, oddly sitting with his right hand comfortably grasping on a glass of red wine.

He's wearing a different kind of outfit, compared to the one I last saw him in. I've got just the right phrase for his new look. *Boujee* in white.

That grey chair he's sitting on, I don't think that belongs in my room.

Is this a dream? Because if it is, this sure feels like it isn't.

"What are you doing here?" I scream loudly for everyone in the house to hear.

His presence surprises me tremendously that my body immediately jumps out of the bed in less than a heartbeat.

By any second, I can storm out of the room anytime I want, as the space between me and him is huge; but somehow, my body doesn't want to leave without his explanation. This is my curiosity taking over, right here right now.

He hasn't really spoken anything again ever since the similar midnight that irritated me. He just keeps sitting there quietly like he doesn't plan to go anywhere else. His eyes draw near, though his body stays still. The way he looks at me, it's rather mysteriously peculiarly scary. With his seemingly favourite red wine swirling around the translucent vessel, I wonder where he got the bottle from.

After a while, his mouth slowly opens for words.

"I didn't do it, any of it," he finally says what is truly on his mind, and on mine too.

"*Primum non nocere,*" he adds.

"Meaning?" I'm wondering why everybody's testing me with Latin words.

"First, do not harm," he responds; and while saying that, he's bringing his body against gravity and slowly walking towards me.

"Well, do you or do you not?" I answer, while forcing myself to stand very firmly on the ground like I'm not going to crack frightened slugs.

"Those that deviate from it do, they mean every harm," he says, "But I am not one of them," his voice is louder as he insists on pleading not guilty.

"Then why are you still hiding?" I scream. "You don't need to if you're innocent," this time, my voice gets tremendously louder right at the last part.

"If you were in the same room where the murder weapon and the body were, and there was an eyewitness right where you left the murder scene with just you and the body; tell me, would you not run? Or would you rather hide until they find the killer, while hoping they would find him sooner than later?"

I'm going to say that there's nothing to be afraid of as long as you're innocent; but now that he puts it that way, I start imagining putting myself in his shoes. I'd probably do the same, except that there would probably be a lot more running involved as I'd risk myself getting caught just to investigate myself.

"But I'd at least find a way to tell them what I really saw," one can never underestimate a good bluff.

"Well, I'm not going to risk that. Didn't you see my sleeping pills? I've already had so much stress just to hide from my patients, my obligations, and now the whole world; not to mention adding that risk to my misery."

"Where are you hiding, then?"

My heart beats so fast I don't think it even skips a beat, two at least.

"I'll show it to you."

In a mere second, we arrive at a place so empty. It almost looks like a void in the universe. I don't think such whereabouts ever exist in the real world.

"Where is this place?"

"My house," he responds.

My eyes get so big from my inability to process his answer, my heart to almost a disbelief that he doesn't even flinch at such an expression. I guess it's just an obvious reaction, otherwise an absolute corroboration of the doctor's famous quiet trait.

"Why is there none?"

"Because you've never seen it," he answers shortly.

From there, I immediately know what he means, what this all means. Experience serves me well with knowledge.

Accordingly, he then starts to slowly explain to me why this place, why not out there.

There is only one place in this world within his maximum control as a human being, or as far as having a built-in mysterious passage within which he's the only one who knows about it; aside from his mansion's previous owners I suppose. A neighbourhood full of ancestral mansions with a variety of unrevealed histories and revelations, and the one I currently live in is not excluded.

Whereabout within? His answer is only a blank smile at the wind next to him, slowly evaporating through time having swore he would never tell the others and me. He's not even looking at me.

We sit staring at the emptiness, just thinking, and talking within our mind. I must say, this night has been such a strange night. Even after I unbolt the lock of this pair of blue eyes wide open after this deep sleep, his haze has not left the building of my soul.

Today is estimated to be another day tainted with unwelcomed invitation to the blood and miserly imitation of the past. I shove my window blind still in my pyjamas, looking at the guarding policemen; I'm wondering if they can hear me scream from here. Better be safe than sorry, as shown in the utter feeling of safeness both of my parents are constantly showing; with one drinking his morning hot chocolate without trembling while reading the newspaper, and the other humming while watering her colourful plant collection outside. As long as they're safe and sound.

The whole shooting match is full of uncertainties, except for one thing, that I still don't have Detective Jevon's phone number. So now I have to go to the police station again and repeat the administration process; such a nuisance.

"It is compulsory that you stay inside, Miss. We insist," says one of the guards.

Passing through this barrier is a lot harder than I thought. I'd give them the applause for doing their job properly, but this means that I have to find another way to talk to one of the detectives in charge. I go outside again now but for a different reason.

"How can I contact Detective Jevon?" I ask them nicely with a pair of hot chocolate on both of my hands; you can call these bribes.

They look at each other to raise a telepathic discussion through their eyes to see if they shall accept, and after both silently agree on giving in on the temptation of the irresistible warm fuzzy beverages, they contact Detective Jevon for me.

He was on the case, no further explanation of which. I've sort of expected this, but the next one is completely to my surprise. He has actually been planning to visit me to talk about something.

"I've got some *diggings of the past*," he says before he closes the line.

I can't wait.

My legs can't stop moving forward and backward like a little kid sitting on a sofa waiting for her treat. My mind too, as it spins around the disturbing article hoped to be found sooner. It still amazes me how no one ever noticed the similarity; and if some did, why didn't they come forward with this important piece of clue? Thoughts on repeat.

I vary my excitement by walking back and forth without

reason like a mad woman. Detective Jevon arrives much sooner than he promised, but much later than the invisible timer on my wrist. We then sit on the dining table on the first floor much to the confusion of both of my parents who are later successfully being encouraged to watch haphazardly far from the second level. They vote themselves out willingly from the party.

Without thinking much further why he's comfortable sharing all of this confidential information in the form of countless papers, which he seems to have just gathered overnight, he asks me what I see; as if he's voluntarily mentoring me on how to become a proper detective.

A laptop.

"We've just found this half an hour ago. It belongs to one of the defence attorneys representing Corina Bailhache. Guess who?"

He must be talking about Sir Halihan.

Apparently, this one is so peculiar that it was the only one found in a secret safe behind one of the paintings in his study room where he died. I must say, they've done a really good job at finding this. I can imagine the excitement; just snooping around, finding hidden rooms, looking for clues.

"Guess what the password is," he says.

Is this a test? How should I know?

Furthermore, aren't we supposed to save time and not waste it on some stupid game of whether I know the answer or not? Because, of course I know I don't. However, the expression painted on his face suggests that he's dead serious and therefore wants me to think hard. Simply shrugging my shoulders isn't acceptable. I should try my best at the very least.

I'm thinking hard, very hard, harder than ever with both of my eyes wide opened. I see the impatient detective, stay-still furniture, and my mom's colourful garden by the window while pondering. Still nothing.

His presence gives me the pressure, but he doesn't seem like the kind who will take giving up as an answer. Then, I think I've got it, sort of.

"Corina Bailhache?"

"We've tried that one, but it didn't work. We still have one attempt to go."

One?

JUST ONE?!

Why doesn't he just give it to a computer expert in his team to solve? I mean, there's no room for error there. Why does he have to drive all the way here - actually, from Sir Halihan's mansion to here is not that far - and waste his precious time on asking me for the possible password; moreover as his last attempt? I never expected him to trust me that much. Heck, I've never even trusted myself that much.

My heart is racing but suddenly a voice in my head tells me to settle down, and breathe.

"Can I go to my room?" I excuse myself with a question in which I don't even wait for an answer. I don't even glance at his later expression. He'll probably think I'm just giving up, because I just get up and leave.

Here in my chamber, I close my eyes in the atmosphere that suits me best, and really ponder. This bedroom's smell makes me calm. My best thinking can only be done here. All pressure is off me. He can even bring the laptop to his computer forensic team and I won't even care; I think it's best if he does this rather than waiting for me.

Everything is dark; everything inside is moving very fast. Sometimes they are words and other times pictures in motion. They go side by side at first, in a weird way, then they move diagonally from one to another as if they're all doing a trade of position; but then afterward, they disperse randomly. It's all very strange but I guess that's how my brain tries to simplify its process from everything I know for the past twenty five years, searching for relevancies.

I can't believe it. I've got it.

Soon after, they all stop moving then go down vividly like fallen air drops in the nightfall and splash into the ocean; because they touch the water at the same time, they create an explosion sound altogether.

At least, I think I've got it.

I go downstairs and see once again his confused physiognomy. I'm really impressed that he chooses to risk it all and wait for me instead. Before I even plan to say anything, I softly drag the laptop towards me and type with full confidence what I believe is the right password.

I'm clicking Enter.

There's no going back, regardless if I'm right or wrong.

33

§

The Confession

I KILLED CORINA

All the pertinent words with two spaces and all in caps.
And we're in.

The detective is still silent. No praise, no applause; pure drive
of moving on like nothing's wrong colonises his being.

"What would you have done if I had got it wrong?" I
sincerely want to know whether he would throw me up in the
air or fly his punch at me for it, just any painful imagination
I've got left.

"There would still be one more attempt remaining," he
answers.

So, there were two?

This time, I can see him giggling, to my utter chagrin. I didn't know he could be quite funny at times. Maybe that's what attracted Miss Decima to him, some needed humour in her boring loaded life. I don't think her long-life friend - the cigarette - can make her laugh that much, at least consciously.

I should've known. He wouldn't dare to risk the whole investigation just to know if I'm capable of solving it. I can still see him grinning from ear to ear being proud of his illusion; so annoying. But to think that he'd go this length to test me, I can't help thinking if I do have some promising potential in me after all. People in general don't give you more than one chance to prove yourself.

As both of his hands stroll around the keyboard, I stand at the back quite far from the back of his head with both of my arms pretzeling across my chest. Suddenly, within about ten minutes, he manages to find some sort of an auspicious folder, hush-hush from the others.

The name itself is even unchanged. 'New Folder'. Inside, there's only one video.

Based on this, we're able to make up the timing in the timeline when he recorded the video, which is surely before his death, but after my uncle and aunt's.

Play.

"Ahem ahem.

If you're watching this, as I'm *sure* you are right now, that means I'm dead.

I'm dead and I somehow manage to write down the whole phrase as the key to unlock this before I am, well, dead. Be mindful that the secret I'm about to tell you is not one I will bring to my grave upon my death. No, this is my full *confession* for the whole world to witness, only after I'm dead."

Yes, Sir Halihan. You're dead, we got it.

Sir Halihan has both of his arms building fences from the start, with those two windows of his soul lining up straight and gazing sharp against the camera. After giving evidence with his lonely surroundings, addressing that he's doing all of this confession without anyone around and without being forced by anyone, he then grabs some old newspaper. Detective Jevon pauses the video and frantically searches over the paper found in that secret locker, then begins to read the headline.

"Corina Bailhache pleaded guilty to a series of murders, sadly it does not stop there," Detective Jevon reads out loud.

He then clicks play again on the video.

"And once you read them all, you realise you can never unsee the resemblance to the murder of Petunia and Gershom."

"And this is what really happened," he continues.

He tells it so technically structured that my brain can't help but to escape a little bit, imagining a set of stories so close with its own dreamy language.

His story, my words.

Once upon an approaching full moon, a decreasingly manip-ulative lady came in the middle of the night, feeling hopeless.

She trusted that her prerogative was coming to an end; and to ensure her control was transfixed, by a mere blinded judgement she found a sterling man tainted with the lust of silver and gold in the pretence of doing everything in his power only in her best interest. She was convinced to bear a child in a matter of set up, so that her estate would not have fallen to anyone else but her own direct blood.

"This child," Corina said, "would be the only reason."

Little did she know that there had been a lucrative plan in store for half of its blood, foul-natured by the hunger for power and fortunes the paternal was forever vowed into, and surely neither in her estate's nor her best interest - not even the baby's. She knew eventually; as the painful truth was laid out while the shaved crystal of her own method was blown to her nose by the father of her child, he killed her and he left her dead in the hospital in the arms of nobody.

"That child, is my child," Sir Halihan confirms, "and I killed her mother with the same *crystalline metalloid*," he admits while the water dam broke down his eyes and fell as tears on both of his cheeks; the same time he convinces himself proud of being able to match the perfect timing between the labour, the murder, and the burial as soon as possible to have her death committed as natural. I can't tell whether he wants the audience to see him as grieving, feeling guilty, or mere bragging.

"I still needed help for my plan to work," he admits sorrowfully, and I guess full of regrets this time.

Then comes Petunia, the poorest but fairest of the land. She was suppressed for her unreadiness to bear a child, but it was not the truth that she was unable to. This too she kept it hidden, as well as about her poverty she never wanted her closest ones to know, from the slothful prince she obeyed who worshipped her for her snake-hipped figure and motherhood prospect.

The baby plan came just in time, in the promise of a share of fortune that her husband would accept without knowledge; consequently just the perfect time for her to pretend her belly was ready for the baby her husband would never expect to never be his or hers. As long as she would never have to give up her slenderish body for the rest of her life, such rigorous effort in the process would not once be a problem.

Petunia needed help; and it was Lesley, who was on the verge of bankruptcy due to her many mortgages, that came in the plan to survive her own impediment. Her opera days incidentally taught her no less in how to play off the pregnancy pretency very well. There was one more person they needed to take part of the plan, and it was no other than Godric who cared no less about his share of the fortune being tainted by his half-sister's blood.

"After all that was perfectly laid out, all I needed to do was the *finishing touch*, easy enough for me to do," he continues and further sobs.

I can't tell if he's crying out of regret or satisfaction.

Fortunately, the fortunes were more than enough to buy all of them a new start in life, far away from the big city, into the ancient wealthy neighbourhood. Since then, they've been infiltrating the community to avoid suspicion and sticking together living luxuriously with the mysterious fortunes in the guardianship of none other than the only rightful heir to the blood-tainted fortune, Idonia. Yes, whoever is lawfully regarded as Idonia's guardian will be the only one with unlimited access to the Bailhache family fortune, all only lasting until the little girl turns twenty one. It was of course never their intention to let her know the truth.

"The fortune's supreme is understatedly regarded for a purpose, you see. In what manner, one of the many is not to attract any unwanted media attention. Another manner is to keep it hidden from everyone else. That woman, Oriel, if she hasn't found out by now, she's probably one step closer towards; as she too has been relentless in suspecting the mysterious fortune and does all the snooping by and for herself," Sir Halihan continues.

"I'm trying my best to survive, to stay alive; but if the truth ends up killing me, as I believe it eventually will, then so be it."

And he strikes out one last lamenting horrifying smile before the video ends.

34

❧

Secret Family Fortune

Mrs. Lesley Peacock goes inside the interrogation room, as I see her from the invisible window on the other side. The sonorous woman with two adorable plump cheeks and chubby flowered bun looks like she's about to faint off the stage.

"Nothing in the missing suspect's house, no sign of him either. I thought maybe he wanted you to know," Detective Potsy says to me.

He too seems confused as to why I'm allowed to stand right besides him while Detective Jevon and Detective Gervase take on the action behind the glass.

"What?"

Mrs. Lesley says the short word with a long pitching warble that constantly changes notes; she still sings even when she's busted.

"You all have come to my house and asked questions that I have fully answered. What more do you want?" She continues.

"The truth, and if you don't start with that, we will. And when we do, the consequences will be more severe," Detective Jevon sets the scene straight that the singer starts to crumble.

While once in a while sobbing tears, she reveals all the master plans that Sir Halihan, Aunt Petunia, Doctor Godric, and herself have been a part of, which she insists all were with rocketing regrets from her part.

"That Oriel, that woman. She must have known too! Otherwise, she wouldn't have insisted on becoming Idonia's guardian!" Mrs. Lesley screams then half stands up persisting the two detectives to do something about it.

"Maybe she killed them, she killed everyone! For the money! I've known all along she was always trying to get close to Petunia just to know about her mysterious funds; that greedy old-bag, she'd do everything for the money!" She continues while slowly sitting down and mumbles the rest of the sentence.

Where is Mrs. Oriel by the way? I believe she was being picked up too for interrogation but she hasn't shown her face anywhere in this building. Is she still in my uncle and aunt's mansion along with Idonia?

I don't stay long for Mrs. Lesley's interrogation; so instead, I leave to see Idonia to see how she's doing.

"Where is Mrs. Oriel?" I ask Mr. Catullus.

"Oh Miss, she asked the officers to send her home," he responds.

From his expression, I can tell he's irritated by her sense of ignorance towards the little girl. Maybe he does care about Idonia.

Just like that, Idonia is left alone once more.

Without asking for anyone's permission, I bring myself upstairs and knock on her door. The same three times as I did the first time, and instead of giving another try due to no answer, I choose to turn the knob again instead; but this time, it's locked.

"Miss!" Mr. Catullus screams. "I would not if I were you. Did you hear anything, Miss?"

"What do you mean? Is she inside?" I ask Mr. Catullus again as I go down the stairs; more like he politely pulls me away from Idonia's door.

"Hmm, nothing, Miss. She is... she should be... she probably doesn't want to see or talk to anyone, maybe anymore. She tends to do that a lot, Miss."

"Would you like to stay for dinner, Miss?" Mr. Catullus's exceedingly polite words almost tempt me to decide to bail on my later appointment - I don't really have any - and see instead the dishes being prepared this evening.

But I'm more worried about Idonia eating alone somehow. It's not the usual me. The usual me would not care less for her and would choose to stay only for the food.

"I'll stay," I answer; much to his delight, since there haven't been that many visitors ever since.

I can see that Mr. Catullus' heart is really to serve; he seems to enjoy serving here, as well as the rest.

Idonia's better off being taken care of by them, I start to

think. I also know without my presence that even my mom and my dad visit the house multiple times just to vocal their willingness to take care of Idonia if allowed without a war; they still think Idonia is of my uncle's blood. But somehow, that never gets to settle. As my parents themselves are fond of travelling more than the regular often, they don't have the liberal urge to force the idea around the house. She doesn't really have a choice if we coerce her, we all know it; but I guess either we prefer to give her one or none of us actually cares that much.

That rustic timekeeper in the dining room turns its shorter line to six post meridiem, then seven, eight. I wait. However, the door to Idonia's room is neither once unlocked nor opened during these hours. She doesn't even respond to the maids calling and knocking on the door. After a long while, I tell myself that it's time to leave. She's too upset to see anyone.

What a waste of time, but I have no grudge against her. The little girl's behaviour is utterly indescribable, truly unexpected, but the reasoning is highly understandable. I mean, who wouldn't be? Everything is going so fast and so wrong at the expense of her increasing loneliness, and it's just for her family fortune that she doesn't even know about.

35

∽

Under Arrest

"Where have you been?"

Marge screams so loud on the phone but instead of apologising, I tap my lips for I can't help but laugh; she's supposed to shush herself not to wake her children.

We're the same age. I first met her back in school. Her husband is next to her building a memory with their children sleeping on his lap, probably smiling. Meanwhile, I'm not even close at all to getting a boyfriend.

"You were supposed to pick me up hours ago!" My dear friend screams in desperate of her way out to escape her full-time motherhood reality.

I almost forgot.

Every once in a while during the weekend, we have our

cocktail nights. Sometimes we're joined by the others, some-times it's just the two of us.

I'd explain to her my situation; but in fact, I'm just look-ing for confirmation from someone other than myself that it's totally okay if I sneak out. I know the hidden passage like the back of my hand. First, I need to change to a pair of jeans because there's no way I can climb the fence with that fancy silky long beige skirt I was thinking of wearing. Second, I make use of the maids' beauty to approach the officers with some nice hot chocolates. My mom won't like the idea, considering we lost one of them not too long ago from the delivery man when they fell in love, but I have no other choice at the moment. And if they rat me out, I can always deal with the consequences later. Do first, think later; it's always the way to go for me.

I haven't seen these flowery gates for a while, but the grown ivy roots are the ones doing most of my work here. This is easier than years ago when I last climbed on one of these. It's really like climbing a magical stairs; but instead of taking you to a magical land, it's bringing you to one of your neighbour's gardens instead. I think they call it 'trespassing' these days. One of their maids actually does see me coming in, and there seems to be no one else but her. This old lady doesn't even look like she's surprised or scared from my sudden presence; instead, she signals me the way out. I wonder what my neighbour did that crossed her spirit. So thanks to her and the vine, my way is clear and bright as daylight.

Tonight, we're joined by another of us, Patricia. She's a full-time entrepreneur who only joins when she's either too happy or too burned out. She also seems to not have an entirely sober scheme planned out, as she intentionally goes with a taxi instead of her fancy pricey electric car.

"Cheers!" The three of us salute as we then continue to celebrate another hour we're wasting in our prime years.

"We used to be able to do this every night; now, barely once a month," Patricia reveals the truth about our adult society.

We ask each other what has been happening in our life for the past thirty days, since the last time we hung out. Marge, nothing much besides her endless pursuit to get her children to the best school in the country. Patricia, nothing else besides changing her dating partners that varies every month of the year; a good life, she says.

Then, it's my turn to share my stories.

Speechless, until the end. No interruptions but appalling and distressing expressions to their disbelief; the endless actual murder series I witness that usually appear as fiction.

"I have an idea! Why don't we go to the doctor's mansion?" Patricia, appearing to be slightly drunk from two glasses of sangria, suggests her impulsive idea.

"Are you out of your mind? Although, I *kinda* feel like I *kinda* need that sort of excitement in my life too," Marge shows her doubt, but she may be a bit drunk too.

As it comes seemingly for me to decide - we're all actually seeing eye to eye on Patricia's proposition - I choose somewhere between the middle.

All inside with Marge in front and Patricia at the back, we in my car giggle at each other with excitement in the expectation that we'll just see nothing but a dark big house standing tall among the others. The road is empty with no lights, the three of us, the sky with just a little bit of sunlight left before the evening ends; two are quite heavily unsober, excluding myself.

No police. We're heading towards the entrance.

"Now what?" I initiate the conversation, hoping they'll slowly realise that they don't even know what they're going to do next.

"It's not that I don't want to go inside. I'm scared... I've got kids, you know!" Marge screams.

Just seconds after arriving in front of the quiet mansion owned by the missing suspect, she chooses to stay back even in her drunken stage. Based on her bouncing arms, she's suggesting she just wants us to go back to the car. Not until...

Ding dong. Ding dong.

"Who's that?" Marge and I scream unwantedly up to the point that our voice fills almost all of the void in the moving air surrounding us; it could probably wake the neighbours up as we speak.

Patricia giggles. Getting off limit beyond the police line, Marge and I immediately realise that she's the one ringing the bell without our consent. It's obvious from Marge's sombre expression and my shocking ghast that Patricia needs to get home safely before she's doing anything else stupid that she's going to regret for the rest of her life. Of course I'd have done all of this if I was just by myself, but it feels different when it seems like

I'm jeopardising someone else's life. Regardless, we should've expected this to happen when we ourselves began to lose count on how many drinks have been poured out; probably the full liability is solely on me since I wasn't really drinking.

We slowly but surely head back to where my car parked, just in front. I look back quickly before leaving the front porch. I accidentally glimpse at one of the windows on the left and I can't help but notice something... odd.

One of the curtains on the left side sways swiftly lento, just roughly in a span of one hundred fifty five centimetres high point above the ground, and then stops; unlike the rest who seem to have been staying still for the rest of the cold air.

Maybe it's just a picky wind heading towards that particular direction; I encourage myself before I increase the speed of my walk on my way to the car, in which both of my friends follow unconsciously to the acceleration.

I return them safely and soundly back home, then detouring via the same passage. I'm passing once again Doctor Godric's house very very slowly. Only this time, I notice that the light is suddenly on and then off again in a matter of seconds. The time now is almost midnight.

I can't believe what I've just seen. Is that real or am I just seeing what I want to see? Should I call the police? Then, the question leads to the next of whether I do 'the stupid' by coming in myself to check on the situation. I do think I'm not that smart, so I might as well do the stupid thing.

Gulp.

I feel I want to break in without telling anyone first but a wise consciousness inside of me keeps telling me not to. Instead, I do 'the responsible' and call the police; I still can't believe I haven't got any of the detectives' direct lines. I ask for them to immediately stand by the mansion.

In a matter of minutes, three police cars arrive followed by Detective Jevon's and Detective Potsy's cars. Detective Gervase seems not to be coming with this time.

"Are you sure about this?" Detective Jevon raises his question to me as if the presence of numerous authorities, himself included, is not enough to prove to me that he's actually already trusted my instinct that much.

Soon enough, they all - except me - proceed to go inside the mansion with their guns pointing out their front. As for me, I wait outside near my car like a baby. I wish I could come in too; but seeing all of those weapons, I'm somehow certain that I might mess things up then get shot rather than do any help. I can already imagine the bullet being the magnet for my flesh. It's me, so of course the worst usually happens. Probably best if I don't interfere this time.

Suddenly, I hear sounds coming from the mansion. Loud screams.

I can't exactly understand who's screaming or why, but it sounds like they do discover someone they've been looking for.

Bang. Bang.

I don't know what's going on this time but I'm pretty sure it's a gunshot that I've just heard. Then two more.

Who gets shot? Who fires it? Is someone dead or at least injured?

Then I realise they've got it all covered. It's too obvious now.

Two police officers come out of the mansion shortly after the clock ticks to night twelve. As they walk towards their duty cars, three others follow with the middle one begins a slow amble unreluctantly hopeless and whose arms stay taut without mercy from the others as their own wrap around both his shoulders each.

The missing suspect is now under arrest.

It is indeed Doctor Godric Simpkin in the middle.

What a lucky night, the officers must be thinking the same, and what are the odds that I get to see him probably turning on and off the light by mistake at the right time for me to witness. He was probably surprised by the unanticipated bell and lost his grip for a second there, right when I came with my friends.

The face of the man who had been searched for so many days looks rather excruciatingly pale. He's not a missing suspect anymore, but he looks rather missing from the presence of the world; his expression tells me so. Almost like he still feels hopelessly stuck in his nightmare and hasn't got enough strength to bring himself back to reality, which is no different after all. Yes, his face declares all that without a single word spoken as they pass right by in front of me reaching the source of the sirens.

Detective Jevon comes at me, not looking as happy as I thought he would be.

"Potsy's still inside," he gives a voice rather slowly.

"You see," he adds; but then he pauses with both of his arms on both sides and his face looking down, leaving me wondering without any idea what the heck is still going on in there.

Is there somebody else in there?

His upper lip tweaks a little as he looks up to me and says, "There's another body in there, fresh," without a further name.

With a beyond curious instinct, I go inside immediately to confirm what I've just heard. I want to confirm the identity that's spoken by his eyes, and see if my gut tells me it's who I think it is.

And it is indeed, a she.

36

❦

Blessing in Disguise

I'm walking towards the back of the house that leads me to the garden. From a long way of sight, I can already sense a quiet figure near the door. What's worse, I also smell the freshness of blood.

The body lies hopelessly on the wooden ground just between the aperture. Both of her hands are lining straight passing her head. Her long skirt trails on the blooded rail showing that she had been dragged against her will to where she is now.

It is Mrs. Oriel Walmsley, with an inhabited bullet hole on her chest.

But how could she be here? I thought the officers had taken her home safely, plus a bunch of others were watching over us in front of our house. I guess unless we didn't want them to be - obviously relatable to me - and for that ourselves were to blame. Since I could even still have my girls evening out with no problem, maybe she got her own hidden passage planned out too. So now, I don't even know if it is the system or the actuality that is to blame. It makes more sense to me that she came out secretly of her own accord, so the reason is the one that still bothers me.

Those tepid-looking crime scene investigators finally arrive. Despite the little enthusiasm shown on their face, they're moving and doing their own thing like a super-smart robotic vacuum. As for me, I don't really know what to do. Here I am, minding my own business without being forced to leave the murder scene like I used to. It's funny that when I'm not put up against the pressure of constraint, I don't really know where to start. Why does one's brain seem to work more efficiently at the brink of disobedience?

I'm just standing here in the corner like a statue, pretending to be thinking seriously while looking at this garden; which reminds me, this garden smells a bit odd, almost like it has this smell of stinking corpse lily.

"What is this smell?" One of the CSIs seems to agree with me.

As he passes by, he looks at me and the garden, blocking his nose with his right index finger that's covered with white glove. I hope he doesn't think that the smell is coming from me.

"You're not going to believe what I've just seen!"

One of the CSIs surprises Detective Jevon and Detective Potsy with her finding. Renae is her name, as Detective Potsy calls out her name proudly and loudly for doing a great job.

She notices a bunch of security cameras around the outer side of the house. There seems to be none inside though, she implies. However, the cameras are so well-hidden as they're camouflaged as a bunch of cubes of I-don't-know materials cemented on the wall. This must be how Doctor Godric managed to escape the arrest before when the officers were searching for him here.

"Finding the *wellspring*, we are working on it as we speak," she says with a big smile and firm grasp on her knuckles, ready to punch. I'm thinking she calls it 'wellspring' as she imagines this premise to be some sort of fantasy land where she's just simply playing hide and seek.

Exhibiting her relentless confidence and competence, I must believe I need to learn from her just how. In just a mere few minutes, not far from where the body was, she manages to find a gun inside a bin near the back of the house. Same woman. God, how does she keep doing it?

However, two hours have passed and there is no sign of them ever finding the hidden whereabouts. First floor, second, then third - the efforts implicitly suggest that the investigation may soon come to an end. To me personally, the house seems to be like an immeasurable escape room with visible enigmas; this I only need to pay by the hour with my time for the excitement.

I'm trying my best of course. I'm searching through the deep of the ground and shallow of the sky of this mere premise but it reaches to no lead. Where can it be?

The walls are bared and the concrete is probed but nothing suggests somewhere here is where the masterplan is hidden. Some find access into one or two hidden grounds but end up coming out with false hopes; those only lead them to mere bric-a-brac and white elephants, seemingly-junk artefacts with questionable sources and originality. Doctor Godric is apparently an underground hoarder. But I must admit, he seems to have a rather exquisite taste for ornamentations.

The building which seems to be dominated with schematic green out of peculiarity of the owner does wonder to everyone who enters for the first time; but as soon as we stay for longer than we hope, even the profligated pillars and lavish statues for a taste are not enough to compete for our longer attention. Our only objective is to find the missing puzzle.

"No luck?" Detective Jevon suddenly surprises me with his comment from behind.

"Not yet," I give the response with a low voice, disappointed with myself for disappointing him; classic people pleaser, and I'm not even getting paid to be here.

"Any news from Detective Gervase?" He asks one of the men next to us who's still swinging each painting on the wall in this first floor corridor.

This man has been doing so for the past few hours; I came across him before. I heard he was in Sir Halihan's residence too when they found that secret safe. Finding a secret passage behind paintings seems to be one of his strengths behind his most ordeal, because clearly he doesn't enjoy it. I swear I saw him smacking the low point of these paintings at one point that they were swinging far and wide helplessly. He thought nobody was watching. Maybe he's just tired, maybe he's disappointed with himself too; at least he's getting paid to be here.

"No Sir, he hasn't got anything out of the suspect."

Turns out Detective Gervase is already on the clock too, interviewing Doctor Godric.

Weird. My usual self would probably speed to the station and barge in the interrogation room out of curiosity; but no, I don't really want to right now.

"You seem tired. Why don't you go lie down for a minute in one of these chambers? Officer, show her that grand one on the first floor," Detective Jevon suggests, very much to my relief.

It's odd, and it's almost morning; not that it makes any sense, which means I'm not even making sense any more. I feel so tired that I begin to leave any credibility I've built just to lay on one of these velvet beds with lenient white curtains. I need to rest. I don't even get paid for doing all of this. I think to myself in my circumstantial prejudiced attitude as my fatigue starts to take control, which I'm sure I'm going to regret when I wake up.

I look at my phone and even my parents haven't messaged me anything today. They probably think I'm still in my bedroom reading the whole day, so they haven't been worried sick. They're probably asleep by now and they must be sleeping comfortably knowing those officers are still outside watching the house. They very much like the idea of 'the more safety, the better'.

As my head touches the strange silk of the pillow with my earpods, it seems that I'll be sleeping just *not* fine. Luckily I always bring these earpods around, so I try to squeeze them tighter in my ears, but it seems that the effort just adds to my existing nuisance. Could be the classical music through my ears or the endless conversation to myself, but I think the idea of many officers and CSIs running around the house is the main reason my embodiment doesn't spark comfort for my forty winks.

So I'm once again face to face with the blue indoor sky on top. Besides, the idea of my body resting in a stranger's bed seems to be just enough for now to bring myself against the cloud, completely still being aware of the reality around me.

If I were Doctor Godric, where would my hiding place be?

There's not much I know about him though. I should better leave it all to Detective Gervase to let us know the answer, as the rest of the others are seemingly starting to think of that. It'll save so much time if he can just quickly spill the whereabouts and stop us from staying here longer than we want.

Still, if I were, so to speak, where would I?

If he had been hiding in his mansion like I presume, which hasn't even been confirmed yet, then probably the location of the secret passage would be in the room he'd feel the safest too, somewhere he could also gain maximum control in.

Where would that be if I were him? Study room? Bedroom? Bathroom?

And what are the three basic living principles that a hidden room should be able to provide? Let's see. Food, clothes, and a roof. Supply of nutrients, bathroom for hygiene, and sheltered space with proper air circulation. Those would be my top three criterias to stay hidden and sane at the same time. And eyes, of course, around the house. The access is there for sure - we've all already suspected it.

But where, where would it be? Would it be below the ground or above the ceiling?

I step out of the bed and surge through the sea of crowds with their brushes and guns. They can probably tell I'm giving up on sleeping. I commit myself to do as many, many, many, weird deportments. Sleeping is not working for me anyway.

I begin with the study room. With lots of books and under-pin statues, I begin to push back and forth every book on the shelf and every sculpture ever exists in this very room. That would be very *cliché*, wouldn't it? After giving, not just the books and statues, but almost all of the objects in this room a really good shove and pull moments, it becomes more and more apparent to me that this room is just not it.

Next stop is the kitchen and living room altogether. Same thing. I push and pull most of the objects in the room until my hands are getting tired of trying. My steps are more than ready to move on to the next. Same thing with the music hall, three bathrooms, a few untouched bedrooms I don't even want to ask why they look the way they are before my headache comes back, and even the stinky garden.

We've all been pretty much exhausted and the clock has just turned to eight ante meridiem; this exact hour my mom calls me in a rage and broadcasts in a loudspeaker the whole crime possibilities that mostly happen to women who disregard their well-being by not coming home. Surprisingly, this time she actually succeeds to terrify me to my every bone. I think I have to agree with her, this is a good time for me to get home.

Oh yeah, where are my earpods?

They must be still on that red velvet bed, so I rush there and try to search for them as soon as I can. Up to this point, if I can't find them within ten minutes or so, I'll just have to leave them. Who would want to waste precious time for my earbuds?

I don't know what's going on with Doctor Godric but I'm more quizzical as to why the police haven't got him to talk. I always reckoned that would be faster.

I begin to have a feeling that those missing earpods travel under the bed. It's such a narrow space under the bed that my hands can barely reach anything in the middle. I scan my surroundings and look for something that I can use to assist. Probably something long and skinny enough to go through underneath. I don't know, something, something...

A guitar? That would work. Also, I didn't know Doctor Godric plays. But then again, I don't really know him that well anyway; that shouldn't be a surprise to me.

I 'borrow' the guitar from the side of the wardrobe and begin to swing it across the surface underneath the bed, hoping that somehow those two pods will just swift through to the outside.

Grlk. Grlk. Grlk.

Something... something is moving.

Ouch! Something hits me.

Oh wait. The bed is moving!

I suddenly realise what's going on as the side of the bed punches my forehead. If my body is not quick enough to leap to the back and plod backwards with my butt, there's a very high chance that half, if not all, of my body could be stuck underneath. Not that it'll squeeze my body half, as it turns out. Below the bed, after such nether mechanisms flow, there's a square hole that fits perfectly for one person to go down the ladder into the current unknown.

One of the officers who just happens to pass the room I'm in sees my breakthrough and so he proceeds immediately to have everyone in this room right away by screaming the announcement from just outside the door. Once again, I seem to find something useful by accident - mere accident in my honest truth. As it appears, I had the guitar *by accident* switch on a very small red lever on the lower right side of the wall from the middle. My earpods missing was a blessing in disguise after all.

That same officer, Vince is his name, goes down the ladder and up again to tell everyone that it's safe. I'd have gone first, straight away, if he hadn't seen me first.

Vince witnesses a big chamber, even bigger than the room on its head, fit for everyone altogether. But the new problem now is the time it's going to take for everyone to go in and out, as the hole only allows us to go up and down the ladder one by one based on its size.

Detective Jevon, Detective Potsy, a few CSIs, and I are the next in line to finally go into the secret chamber. We see the others meddling around the room, which is clearly Doctor Godric's hideout all this time. The room is like a small one-floor house from the ancient past with about six months of food supply, judging by the tower of canned foods. Seeing all these empty sleeping pill bottles and mountains of such substances, the man is probably still a dead man sleepwalking. I almost give those meds a touch when Detective Jevon suddenly hops on next to me, telling me not to.

I must say, Doctor Godric is very smart. Seeing no electricity and water line whatsoever attached to the area, no bill can ever be related to whatever is used around here. He probably took a dump in the garden upstairs once he saw everyone left. Oh right, that explains that weird smell from the garden. Disgusting.

"You already thought it was going to be Decima, didn't you?" Detective Jevon surprises me and smiles widely at me.

"What do you mean?"

"That day, when I thought it was going to be Idonia as the next victim."

"Oh, I guess. I *suppose*, by accident."

"And I *suppose* this is, too, an accident?" He says it with a gush of heart-warming energy; he really does smile a lot at me these days.

"Actually, yes," I answer shortly as I'm too lazy to think of a better response.

That's just a classic me, being unexplainably cold as people are becoming warm towards me. But perhaps I'm just too scared of losing this warmth if I'm trying so hard to keep it. My mind always wins playing tricks on me.

Detective Jevon then explains to me how he also trusts me back then about my hypothesis in regards to Mrs. Oriel being the next victim; not a hundred percent, he adds. But let's just say, if there's an election between Mrs. Oriel and the others, he'd also choose Mrs. Oriel as the answer. He could already guess from the first interview.

Would he still trust me if I say my gut still doesn't believe that Doctor Godric is the culprit, even after all this?

"Sir! Come quick!"

Vince screams; soon after, Detective Jevon, Detective Potsy, and me hop just into the next side of him.

I can't believe it. We all almost can't.

A few of security monitoring screens playing the footage of Doctor Godric dragging Mrs. Oriel's dead body inside of the house towards the garden outside, with clearly a gun in one of his hands. It's the very same one that he later threw into the same bin where it was found. He's caught right with the very same security cameras he had installed for his sake.

"Jackpot," Detective Jevon bellows out the master stroke with a pair of his eagle eyes. "Imagine if I never asked you to sleep up there."

Oddly, sometimes I can't help but wonder, what if there's no coincidence and that he has instead been the culprit all along?

37

Where's the Crystalline Metalloid?

"I didn't do it!" Doctor Godric screams as he finally wakes up from his sleeping pill.

It turns out to be the reason why he hasn't been able to communicate properly in answering his secret chamber whereabouts - what else is the reason anyway. Not that it matters anymore, especially seeing how scary Detective Gervase is looking right now with his organised thick eyebrows and mammoth muscle serving willingly as his assistance to his advantage, demanding Doctor Godric's utmost confession to the hard evidence involving my uncle's very own gun in his hand. Just to cheer him up a little from here; I wasn't even aware that my uncle had a gun.

"Gervase is one of our best," Detective Jevon murmurs proudly beside me.

That poor guy; if I'm able to speak for him. He's practically down under his knees, considering how he's constantly talking about the future of his medical career, how hard he's been working for it, and of course his potential life sentencing - that is if we assume he won't be getting the death penalty.

"Where is the bell? Where is the rope? Where is the poison?" Detective Gervase screams at the doctor's defence.

"I don't know what you're talking about!" Doctor Godric continues to cry out loud. "I don't even have any idea how the *real* killer can get his hand on the arsenic," he continues.

"How did you know about the arsenic being the right type of the poison?"

Oh no, the *guilty knowledge information*.

But he did suspect the substance from the beginning, even I did. I mean, he is a physician; actually, he might even have access to it - but that doesn't make him the killer straight away! I'm waving my invisible pom pom right now.

But the more I witness his interrogation, the less my brain thinks of him being innocent. I mean, think about it, Daedalia. All of the evidence is pointing out on him, so how can you still think that he is not the culprit? How?

And it's like my heart is now telling me, that is exactly why he's not the culprit. *Everything* is pointing at him.

"You'll know I'm not! Today, there's going to be another killing, I'm sure, while I'm here. You'll feel sorry for me that I'm even here when that happens!" Doctor Godric pleads his innocence, but the detective in front of him doesn't even flinch at the idea of him being falsely arrested.

"Then, why did you hide? If you had come forward, and all of these killings after you had gone missing were concluded, wouldn't your name have been cleared by then?"

Detective Gervase's bluffing seems to work, for Doctor Godric only mumbles at himself this time. He follows the mumbles with constant swears on his innocence. Now, he looks like he's completely losing his mind.

Suddenly, Detective Gervase thwacks on the table with a newspaper and points his fingers right where it says 'Simpkin'. All of us behind this unseen window know where this is going.

"Ludmila Simpkin was born out of wedlock! If anything, I was happier than ever that she was killed, so why would I even take revenge on that? She didn't even deserve the name 'Simpkin'!" Godric's answer reveals his dark side of family betrayal that manages to move his freedom ten more steps backwards from innocence, for all we know.

"If anything, you would! Eventually you took part of your half sister's killer's fortune; and just by eliminating the others, one by one, slowly but surely the rest would be all yours. Isn't that where you're getting at?"

"She is not my sister! And I... I... specially to Petunia... I would never!"

Detective Gervase is laying every piece of evidence right in front of him again. His own poisoning as well as others', the flying dagger, the gun, and his secret passage withholding; the detective continues defying all of the imaginary alibis the doctor has relentlessly been putting out to craft his innocence; he's stirring them into a guilty confession instead. I mean, I am no detective like him, I have no experience as much as these guys do, so maybe they've been correct all along. Why don't I just open my mind on what's real rather than what if?

"We still need his confession," Detective Jevon's mood suddenly changes afterward.

"Why?" I ask.

"And the murder weapon that is able to connect him to all of the murders, the poison. *The crystalline metalloid.* Today too, there's supposed to be another murder, if he's somehow not the killer. Is he really the killer?" The cornerstone of his arms to his chin is fixed on responding to his own question and not mine; his own theory in jeopardy.

In the end, it always comes to the source of that substance being brought up, again.

38

~

The Little Boy

How time flies so fast.

Ten days have passed now since Doctor Godric's arrest, without any more murder as it was supposed to, that the circumstances of him being the culprit have never been stronger. Everyone up to this point believes that he is the killer and celebrates. While waiting for his upcoming trial that he is to be charged for the five murders and one attempted, everyone too comes back to their peace including my parents who choose to leave for a couple of weeks overseas to visit my brother for some leisure escape from the dark age, except me.

Yes, I still somehow have a strong feeling that this is not yet the end. No, not even close.

Madame Hilda Johnson, Mrs. Lesley Peacock, Miss Decima

Somerset, Idonia Pavirsia, Detective Jevon, Mr. Catullus, Adelle, Catherine, Lothar, Rayner, my mom, my dad, and myself. The list goes on and on, and this is only if I still assume that there can only be one murderer. Could it be more?

Today, I pay Miss Decima a visit at her mansion. It feels like it has been quite a while since the last time I saw her, since all of this witnessing dead bodies act encourages my soul to have more contact with the living.

She seems happy to see me, but in a more reserved kind of way. She looks like she's still grasping the fact that she has just skipped her own death.

We have our afternoon tea looking at her bright coloured garden with many rocks assembled to both left and right from the baby size to adult forming a flower bridge over the small pond. The golden fresh air around us helps a lot in making the conversation a little bit more homy, and by golden I mean rare because she isn't smoking around me. But that's a smart move. Who would, if they just happened to be poisoned with traces of arsenic being put in their own cigarette? At least Miss Decima seems to have learned a lesson or two for her own good this time.

"Figured, I've heard about the case," she says with, this time, herbalist smoke scattering around her from her cup of tea.

I form the courage to ask her; why did she look so shocked when she heard that Sir Halihan died? Of course, everyone would be. But no, that expression of hers, it wasn't the usual shock. The shock was definitely something else, a rather 'expected' shock.

"You see, I hold something quietly of his, that he took

quietly from me, that belongs to ME. I just happened to take it right before he died," she answers, to my surprise.

Could it be the...

"And no, that has nothing to do with the case; before I worry you any further," she adds.

Not that it relaxes my mind whatsoever.

"And what is that?"

"And that... I cannot tell you," she answers with a glowing smile that is supported by the beam of the sunlight.

Sometimes, I don't know whether I should keep trusting her or not.

"About my missing credit card, do you think the killer might have taken it?" This time, the sunlight still shines onto her lips but no longer with her smile.

"Do you still remember where you have misplaced it?"

"Not sure. I didn't really give it a thought because it wasn't a big deal for me. People lose their *CC* all the time, you know. Now that I try to remember it, I think it was during my last visit to your late uncle and aunt's mansion. I remember I left my bag on the back porch, because I wanted to walk around the garden, to, you know."

She continues her story on how she got sick of the social force that her escape to the mansion's garden was necessary to clear her polluted mind, with polluted smoke. There were also about five times of her mentioning about seeing a glimpse of the old gardener on her way there and back, Wilbert Cruikshank, that we start to think if perhaps, there was a chance that he was the one who took it. Maybe?

But that doesn't make any sense. He's dead. And if he indeed took it, why bought the crystalline metalloid? Unless, he perhaps killed himself with it? By accident, maybe?

We keep talking about more possible suspects as the thief in mind, but the idea about Wilbert being the thief keeps getting stronger and stronger. He was seen around the porch, the garden, and everywhere she could think of.

With her connection, we decide to search for Wilbert's remains. It appears that all of his belongings were buried alongside him, and it takes longer to get permission to dig his grave. Somehow, she manages to pass all those barriers just within two days, in the sincere excuse of finding the truth, including his death. But she also said a hefty amount of cash had to be involved unavoidably. Of course, this is still a world where money can solve anything for the living.

We are witnessing the dig course of action to our volunteers of mere presence as we speak. One little boy is participating from a long distance, and I'm more than positive that I'm finally seeing in person Tamerlane Cruikshank, the one Adelle talked about. A dinky portion of the earth is taken on and off the giant spade, to reveal a flat hollowed wooden base that is later lifted towards the sky as the goal of the three paid helpers is settled for the day.

We cannot bear to see the corpse for long; as the dreadful smell from it has also started to travel with the wind, Miss Decima asks them to remove all of the belongings quickly and bring the corpse straight back to a *very late* autopsy. Better something small than nothing at all, better late than never.

On a small tent, our hat of very similar trend is twisted on the same side to the right, showing our preparedness to scrutinise these findings. Out of context, I can't help but notice the similarities between my fashion and Miss Decima's. But I need to focus, back from my own source of distraction that is myself, and I physically shake my head as a silent consensus.

"My credit card!" Miss Decima shouts, after only roughly five minutes rumpling the bag of the poor old deceased.

As for me, nothing useful I can find other than these small half-cut rocks swimming alongside various tools in one the boxes. The rocks seem to be of different kinds too.

Suddenly, Miss Decima touches the back of my palm.

"That... could it be... one of them... that *crystalline* stuff?"

Now that she has my attention, I think she could be right. But where is the other half?

We drive afterward with all of these crucial pieces of evidence in my trunk; it now looks as if I was the real mastermind. I immediately park just outside the entryway of the police station after arriving.

Miss Decima looks rather more excited as shown by her brighter complexion from her smile which seems to appear more often these days; good for her. Maybe because she hasn't been smoking. Smoking doesn't do her any good. In fact, it just makes her look older and ruthless.

Detective Jevon seems to have already waited for us at the front. Maybe Miss Decima gave him a call on the way.

Oh! Speaking of calling... nevermind. I can probably get his number afterward. Besides, I don't think I might need it anymore. It's not like there's going to be any murder happening around me again; I sincerely hope.

As we expect, the stone is indeed *crystalline metalloid* but none of them including Detective Jevon seems to find our findings matter and relevant. They seem to be pretty much locked up on the idea of proving Doctor Godric guilty.

"Probably Godric stole it and used it instead," Detective Gervase argues.

"Don't you want to know why this gardener had this in the first place?" Miss Decima shouts quite louder than the rest of the room, bringing the blonde as the centre of attention - an attractive kind though.

"What matters is that we might be able to connect this to him. I'll ask the CSIs to get all of these to trace," Detective Potsy then has all inside the box analysed for the trial, which they hope will bring them to the advantage side in the court.

"What a waste," Miss Decima mumbles to me while letting ourselves out the door with a lesser level of hope than when we started.

I agree with her disappointment. They don't even seem to care if that poor gardener was killed by Doctor Godric or not. Maybe too much on their plate.

We continue our journey by walking to a small cafe just across the station, which we both have never been before. It's not until I see the same familiar figure of a little boy standing outside the police station over there that I impulsively decide to leave Miss Decima alone.

She currently bellows at my vamoose; I run to where the boy is.

I'm glad I'm not hit by a car.

"Hi! Are you...Tamerlane?" My unsteady breath, while bowing with my palms landing on both of my knees from the unplanned running, follows afterwards.

The boy looks perplexed as he unintentionally nods, almost like he desires to run as fast as he can but the whammy keeps both of his feet on the ground, curious about who I am. I invite him to sit in the cafe with me and the still-heavily-confused Miss Decima. After a few polite forces, he agrees to, much to my pleasure.

He looks down to the view of his thighs all the time, but all of that changes when he sees the two portions of burgers as well as fish and chips - each served just for him.

"I have never had this much food before, and for this I must say thank you," the little boy courteously speaks before digging in the dishes of joy in front of him. He even sounds more educated than most of the old money people around here.

I smile at his response, but Miss Decima across me still looks a bit startled and unused to the good deed she's just been a part of. She is more perturbed when I whisper about the identity of the boy, as shown by her widened gaze of expression.

We wait patiently until the last source of carbs and proteins are wiped clean from the plate by his appetite. We offer take-aways for him to bring to his family, much to his eternal delight that the chair he's sitting on almost bounces backward from his stagnant jump of excitement.

This is why sometimes I don't trust my nurtured instinct. As much as it seems that I take him inside out of pity, and as much as I want to believe so, I'm quite sure that my mind has a hidden agenda behind the seemingly good deed exercised. I want information, that's it. I'm feeling really bad about this but I'm still wondering when the right time will be to fulfil that part of my curiosity in me.

"So tell me," Miss Decima suddenly speaks out, "Tell me about your grandpapa."

Miss Decima looks at me thereafter with a knowing smile and a wink that manifests her same thinking to me.

Tamerlane's shining face begins to set at dawn again, but he finally eagerly speaks when Miss Decima tells him that she wants to help him catch the bad guy who did 'bad things' to his grandfather.

He starts by describing the beauty of the garden that his grandfather had passionately grown for his ungrateful masters who never seemed to appreciate him or any of the flowers. He then explains the deceased's peculiar interest in chemistry.

"But only when the stuff is important for the garden," he adds.

I'm no gardener and I know nothing about planting, but I don't think that arsenic would be a good substance to any crops. Then again, I don't know that much about plants.

"Do you know about arsenic?" Miss Decima bluntly raises

her question, much to my surprise and an old man behind her, because she doesn't keep her voice low.

"No. What is that, Miss?" The polite boy responds to this bold frightening lady across from him who's sitting next to me.

"Then, do you know about *crystalline metalloids*?" She amends her question.

Once again, the old man behind her shifts his head towards Miss Decima and goes back with a shake to his head. Crazy lady, he must think.

"No, Miss," he sees towards me briefly when responding, then looks down again.

Miss Decima asks him a bunch more questions later on, but the boy in response repeatedly shakes his head to the sides, every time. Although I'm not exactly sure about her way, I think I know where she's going with this. After some failed attempts, she re-phrases the same questions she asked before; but the one thing she really wants to know, as clear as daylight, is to see if his grandfather teaches him anything in relevance to the poison.

This little boy cannot be the culprit, right?

"Grandfather showed me once," I think he thinks he's whispering but we can actually hear him just about clearly.

"Your grandpapa showed you what?" Miss Decima quickly responds with an enduring smile as it seems that her aimless technique is finally working.

"How to shave one of the crystals. The little *Miss* saw it too. We saw it together, once," he reveals.

"Little Miss... Idonia?" I try to justify, and he nods by degrees in response, very much to our surprise.

Miss Decima and I take little Tamerlane to his house in her car, where we eventually arrive at a tiny homestead with patches and holes. We cannot imagine how a single person let alone three family members live in such a place. The living is undeniably rough. He very much takes his time to let himself out of the car, as the divan in Miss Decima's backseat is much more pleasant than the cold floor he usually sleeps on. Not until her driver comes out and swings the door politely outward that he has no other choice but to come out willingly.

It's evening and I nearly reach home from Miss Decima's house, still in confusion. We all do. And yes, the case seems to form a much bigger conundrum everytime a new piece of information is revealed. More fortuitous and out of the blue.

My car waves into its base and it has come to my intention that a four feet eleven figure is standing at my front door. Her skinny figure slightly moves against the strong wind as she tries to keep her little brown suitcase intact onto her grips. I have no other choice but to approach.

"Catullus said you were looking for me?" She asks while looking up at me as she is just slightly taller than the height of my upper waist.

"Mr. Catullus said that? Well, yes, I was. But how did you even get here?"

"I walked of course. This house is not that far from where I live."

I know it's not that far, but I still don't think that it's that safe of a trip for a small little girl to embark alone on foot at sundown.

"Alone? Why doesn't anyone come with you or let you in?"

"I've just got here, you see," she responds to my worry.

"By the way," she continues, "Would you like to be my guardian?"

The sound of ka-ching fills my ears, but I don't feel at all happy.

39

The Blueprint

I don't know if I should be happy or feeling the other way, but the face of the little child in front of me looks exhausted from being tossed and turned around by many on the weight of fortunes in her name. Most likely she picks me under the excuse that I'm just wandering around minding my own business while once in a while questioning how she's doing. That's probably her definition of genuine caring after all the ignorance from her surroundings this little girl has been fully exposed to. As for me, I'm pretty sure I don't actually care about her that much in the first place.

As much as I've exhibited towards her at least half-pint amount of caring in the account of pity for the last few weeks, I'm still not entirely sure if I'd accept. Heck, what do I know about raising a child? I even still live with my parents; although, that's not such a bad idea. Technically, they'd probably do most of the part in raising her and I'd be much less proactive to do the matter.

One thing that I'm sure of, this kid has a mind of her own. Once she steps into my house, she knows exactly what she wants to do. The first thing she does is to choose her own guest room. My parents have around eight around here, and she goes through each one of them at least twice before coming up with her own decision - one with the view of the left side of this house next door filled with props such as white palace bricks, noble horses as well as varicoloured greens, right on the second floor.

"Do you like the view of Mrs. Lesley's mansion? It's quite, ahem, interesting," I try to sense the idea behind her choice.

"It is," she confirms shortly before she proceeds to load her own suitcase to the side of the bed and freezes looking at me with her hands on top of it; it's a sign for me to voluntarily leave to give her some privacy in her unpacking, apparently.

Two days later.

Another seemingly regular night comes and I meditate on my bed of a plan for the two of us to do the next day. I feel bad that I had to leave her for many hours yesterday to hang out with my friends, though I hurriedly came back in the evening. We've been doing nothing productive other than watching movies together with our pyjamas, which she seems to enjoy very much with me. Considering she'll start her first day with the governess here tomorrow, I wonder if she's sleeping well on this very quiet night.

Wait, what was that?

I thought I heard something, an indescribable blare in which the sound I can't even seem to pronounce at the top of my head. I'm not quite sure. It's like, there's something moving on the ceiling.

I stand up speedily to get out of my bed and grab my dusty tennis racket from the side of the wardrobe. It's been covered with some white powder dusted off by the beauty mirror table next to it. I shake it just a little and get on one of my chairs in the room to knock on the ceiling.

The voice is getting louder and moving to the other direction; I consequently jump to chase it. I'm waving my racket towards the ceiling with gestures proven useless to the obvious eyes. The quick kinetic sound of the source gets louder and louder until my hunt for the ghost sound stops right in front of the room where Idonia sleeps.

Knock. Knock. Knock.
There is no sound.

Click. Click.
The door is locked.

Worried extremely, I call out her name to make sure she

responds, but there is no response except from two of my parents' maids downstairs who're now running upstairs to the second floor. They're catching up with the noise and now arriving where I'm standing.

"Durcel, can you get the spare key?"

"Yes, Miss, right away," and as fast as a bolt she runs to the first floor alone, while Mia hides behind my back.

As Durcel manages to win the running marathon of the night, and just when I'm one click away from unlocking the door, I hear a scream. A scream so loud that Durcel and Mia fall to the ground immediately and beg me not to open the door.

"Stand back!" I scream as I insist on saving Idonia.

I'm twisting the knob.

To my ultimate shock, and what I'm certain will be Durce and Mia's absolute traumatism, we see what we've never seen before. Idonia, almost like she falls from the mid air, standing and jumping on top of the bed fighting something with her own hands. The way she moves, it's like something is diagonally twisted and grasping hard onto her neck.

I quickly rush to flip the nearby switch. When the light rules the space, she sits down on her bed, stupefied by the whole harrowing scene. Durcel and Mia, unlike me, choose to stay just outside near the door. They're still making sure vocally at every step that I make forward towards Idonia's bed that they're there if I need them. Thanks anyway.

"What's going on?" I sit beside her with both of my hands waving up and down near her back and front. Just checking.

"My mom, she came," she responds softly, but loud enough for Durcel and Mia to hear.

In response, the two lovely maids scream. They somehow already get the full picture about who's Idonia's biological mother; must be from my mom.

But there must be a rational explanation about this whole situation. There's no such thing as a *ghost*, right?

As I slowly recall Adelle's paranoia, this must be what she means by 'some nights' and 'spirit voice'. So should I open my mind solemnly on the whole possibility of this... perhaps... I really can't believe I'm saying this... 'ghost'?

The hysteria, everyone's hypothesis; Corina never likes it when her movement is disturbed so she tries to kill her own daughter; but we were just trying to convince ourselves with a speedy answer that Corina really came here as a ghost. But I still don't believe it, not even one bit. It doesn't make any sense; not just the killing part, but her existence too.

There's a war between my brain and my heart, whether to believe that such kind of sick paranormal activity really does exist. Durcel and Mia obviously believe it already. But I'd rather stick to my gut that there must be some logical explanations behind all this that make perfect sense scientifically. I just need to be the one that's making better sense here.

"My mom; she didn't try to kill me, she was just trying to tell me something," Idonia whispers only to my ears. "It was you, wasn't it? Everyone says that you are. That excavator; it wasn't just an accident, was it?"

My eyes are wide open. If she had said this before I had this seed of confidence in me, I'd have probably gone to the police station now and surrendered myself miserably. But no, no way. Where's this even coming from all of a sudden? Who's been feeding her with such thoughts? I bet it's Madame Hilda.

"I saw you," she adds, but she doesn't look at all scared. "But it's okay. You're just trying to protect me, just like my mom," she keeps on hugging me.

What is she talking about? If anything, everything was just an unfortunate knot of mistakes and coincidences tied by my bad choices. The one that was dead was probably just me; who says insecurity doesn't kill? And the ones that skipped my attempted murderous acts were my surroundings who trusted me, witnesses to my wasted potentials, for I never once believed in myself like they did.

"Idonia, how did you–"

Clang. Clang. Clang.

What was that?

While the two maids are hugging each other even tighter, also while screaming at the top of their lungs, I'm sensing the source of the sound coming from the top of the wardrobe. But suddenly, the cover of the vent falls off.

"The ghost must be going through there!" Durcel screams her opinion.

"Or the screw is just loose," I respond as I try to handle all of this freakish situation.

"Make sure to call the repairman to fix this in the morning," I add.

Both nod wordlessly while never once letting go of each other's arm wrapping around their neck. They look like two boxes of gifts tied with one single ribbon.

The next day, the governess comes here instead as Idonia chooses to do so.

A different governess. What happened to the previous one? Did she quit?

The adult introduces herself to me as Miss Sulley, then gives me an estimated time of five hours or so in the study room.

"I'm going out in the meantime. Would that be okay for you?" I was afraid she would not like the idea but from her warm smiling nod, I take it as she has no issue with that.

Instead of letting myself out of the house, I go back to Idonia's room that is just a few steps away from mine. I lock the door just in case the little girl suddenly comes in. I climb up the wardrobe by building myself a temporary staircase from the stockpile of drawers within, until I finally reach the purposeful hole on the wall.

Nothing.
There's absolutely nothing inside.

I've finally fulfilled my word about going out. My car is safely parked right in front of my late aunt and uncle's mansion. There's no one greeting me at the front as no one expects me or anyone to arrive in this house. Now, I'm wondering what they're all doing while the only master left is nowhere to be found.

Adelle greets me with a big smile.

"Is Idonia here?"

"She is upstairs, Miss," she answers my question.

What a total lie.

As I reveal to Adelle that Idonia's definitely not upstairs, she rushes to Mr. Catullus. As a result, the white cloth he's holding on to falls onto his shoes. He quickly grabs the master key to open the door and find her empty room. As much as I want to believe that this is all just them acting, it's even more than hard for me to believe so, more than Idonia's last night incident. Their squeaking shouts and distressed expressions are looking too genuine by view.

Clearly they didn't know that she's been missing for two days. Tsk. Let us hear the applause. At least they're still keeping the mansion cleaner than ever, I have to admit. Did they even forget to remind Idonia of some nutrients?

"No, Miss, please don't," much to my surprise is the response of many, when I tell them that I should bring her back here.

Then, it is revealed.

The terror of the night I experienced last night did happen a lot often here, but less with the screams as no one around here was ever being carried away or courageous enough to go with the pursuit. Much to their superb exhaustion, as they show me the area of the matter - the scene of the 'calling spirit' ritual with traces of burning paper around. The 'ghost', as they call it, first appeared many months ago; and very similarly, any blood-curdling chase always ended in Idonia's room, with the exact paranormal scene. She must have been begging it to come back. If the sound is heard again, they believe that means the time will be coming.

"More blood," they insinuate, as the voice was always heard at least the day before the two murders here, and one on the next.

No one, too, believes it at first; not until they see it with their own eyes.

But I don't. The more I hear about the story, the more I'm sure that this is something real, not a ghost, something truly 'alive' in this realm we call reality.

I go back to my parents' house and proceed my steps to the whirlwinding dusty storeroom as the door is opened for the first time in many years. What I'm trying to find is a blueprint of this mansion. It won't be as easy; I definitely need help but I'd much prefer for Durcel and Mia to keep an eye on those two *strangers* in my study room. This is something I eventually have to do myself.

Found it!

It's actually much easier than I thought. What I'm looking for is just laying there, scrolling nicely on the side of the long table at the back, beside a shiny green-looking ball next to it acting like a flashlight. It's as if it's been waiting for me like a present I deserve.

The room itself is like it had fallen seven feet off the ground; its skyrocketing grotty has shown, and the blueprint looks like it was almost burnt into ashes from the launch. Yes, it's either that bad of a condition or I simply have no idea how to read it. But there was no dust around it.

I bring the blueprint with me quietly as soon as I can to my car. And I put this odd-looking ball in the trunk; I'm very much aware who this belongs to, I just can't think of the reason why. I'm then on my way to Miss Decima's mansion, my seemingly undisclosed partner in this, and she's apparently willing to be a part of it. I honestly can't think of who else to bring this to. And I have to admit, I kind of miss her presence; and by kind of, I really mean really so.

The sunlight and the glass help her face glow even more as soon as Miss Decima sees me from the second-floor window. Meanwhile, here I am worried that the real killer somewhere sees that she's still alive; I've been making my worry shown loud and clear. Just because she thinks she hasn't announced her presence broadly to the whole world, doesn't mean she can just go around the town showing people her proof of living.

Her expression lits up in her study room regardless as she realises what I'm bringing to the table, literally. The woman seems to have been enjoying her hiding in the light at her own dwelling under the false pretence of her suggested coma or death, just to make a long note - still in progress - on who's loyal and who's probably not. She says she knows she has got to be patient, for the time hasn't come for her to reveal herself to the remaining witnesses just yet.

"This is the vent," she points out with true confidence; the snake-looking overlong rectangles slithering across the paper.

We talk for hours. A beautiful lunch of a twisted long appendage derived out of a squid ink pasta dish is even served during our own entourage. What she thinks and what I think about these cases, they're all roughly pretty similar. Her theory is even more engaging, if I'm being honest. I'm thus convinced that she's indeed another quiet observer too, and that fortunately leads to choosing each other as our trusted companion so soon.

Now that I think about it too, for someone who seems to have nothing to do most days of the week, she does have a very high level of knowledge within her brain's possession. I bet she's read all of these books in this room. Books are indeed more honest and easier to read than human beings, I always think.

"What are we going to do about this?" She asks me; as she has read my mind of what I think is happening, as much as she thinks of the same thing too of what is happening.

The breeze in her study room takes cover. We've got it!

We only have about five hours to spare, and we don't even

know yet when, but we think we already know how, and who. No, we don't just think that, we believe so. And we both agree that the real killer is definitely not me. At least, I believe so. Although, I didn't mention to her that little dialogue between me and Idonia.

Idonia saw me.
I mean, what's the relevancy in that?

I did go to the kitchen and passed by the pantry before dinner time, the night Aunt Petunia died.

I did see Uncle Gershom shortly before Doctor Godric did.

About that old lady and the night of Sir Halihan's murder? I claimed I was sleeping at home; at least, I thought I was.

I could just easily slip the poison in Miss Decima's cigarette when I was spending the whole day with her.

And I did go to Doctor Godric's house before the police, where Mrs. Oriel was found dead.

Acting stupid is what I do best, so acting innocent wouldn't probably be that hard.

And the evidence? They're all in my trunk.

But even when everybody's against you, you only have yourself to believe in you.

So I'm really not the killer, am I?

40

∿

The Plan

Five hours to go, before I might die.

"Where's the window?" The lady with a heavy-worn self-made mask asks me with her mind distracted while moving the 'blanket' - her high-dollar scarf all over her head - every two minutes. Her head is spinning around constantly keeping a lookout.

It is of course Miss Decima 'hiding in plain sight'. She has promised to give me pain if I don't let her come along.

"Right there is the study room. You really think we shouldn't call the police yet?"

"We haven't got *concrete* evidence, trust me," she insists.

I believe her, but sometimes I think it's just the many

similarities I see between us that makes me want to really believe her. Though if Miss Decima ends up to be the bad guy here, my naive credence is all to blame.

We know we need to hurry, so we proceed during the day to lead our steps to the dark exit of the confined space at the bottom of the corner, left of the structure. The running air barges into the pulled out aperture as it is set free heavenly, and Miss Decima crawls uncomfortably just underneath the ceiling of the small passage. Luckily she's much slender than me so I don't have to do it. This should have been done the first time we heard about that 'ghost' story. We are indeed the first one to really care about proving its existence.

"I've got it. We'll be able to hear it. Now, hurry!" She yells silently so I run inside as I continue my part.

I rush for next door where Mrs. Lesley lives. Even when knowing that Idonia is currently just next door, she persists in wanting nothing to do any of the sort related to the fortunes of the little girl, let alone taking care of her. She seems to become extremely scared.

"No, Mrs. That's not why I came here. You see, there was this so-called 'ghost', and–"

"Where did you hear the voice this time?"

"You know about the voice?" I'm quite surprised.

Based on a number of worry wrinkles immediately shown on her face, she seems to know about it too. No wonder she doesn't have the ambition to be Idonia's guardian, unlike the late Mrs. Oriel and Sir Halihan; although, let's not forget that she was, too, part of the evil plan at one point.

"Where is this 'ghost'?" Her voice starts to crumble again at every letter.

"I do believe it will be here... tonight, Mrs. Lesley. So... will you let us?"

41

~

The Execution

Three hours to go, before I might die.

The clock almost ticks to nine.

I'm tucked in on my bed waiting for my late night cup of tea. The only music playing is my heartbeat. I'm still wide awake. I've been waiting for a typical kind of sound for a good couple hours now. My senses are wide open to the forecasted surroundings, both Miss Decima and I are expecting, hoping, to evince. But still, nothing.

Two hours to go, before I might die.

Clang.

Oh!

Oh wait. No, not this one. This is just the sound of a plate falling off the floor.

"Sorry, Miss. I seemed to have broken a plate," Durcel comes in with a very strong green tea scent I've been waiting for.

Not going to lie, she almost gave me a heart attack.

"Will you be able to sleep, Miss, with this?"

She seems worried that I'm going to do something that's going to kill me, but my current intention is not to be shared with anyone, at least just yet. I still wonder how long it's going to take for the sound to appear, which should be at any moment now.

One hour to go, before I might die.

Besides the sound of my sweats flowing from my patience running out, nothing.

Then finally, one hour later.

The clock almost ticks to midnight. It should be here by now. Then, there it is. The sound I've been waiting for.

My right ear barely hears the voice, but my left quivers greatly with the magnitude as the little figure goes greatly closer to the source. It's time for me to advance myself to the next setting.

I open my front door and I think I'm almost slipping there. My next view is kind of oozy but I still forcely bring myself to the house next door as I've promised. My nervousness is getting so quick into me, it seems.

I hardly can think of the situation I'm supposed to be in, but it seems harder for me to find the back door Mrs. Lesley has accurately shown me earlier. Fortunately, I still remember where it is, and where I am, after several minutes of delay; but I finally manage to move half step closer towards the next step of the plan, barely, as my knees suddenly pull towards the ground and my palms form a foundation to my linear arms against the floor.

My stomach begins to behave strangely with the blow of nearby air. I have no choice but to postpone my next move for the sake of dropping by the nearest bathroom floor to catapult my misery. The sweats in all my physique are running along with me to my new goal of searching any toilet or sink, whichever nearer. As I coincidentally open one of the bathrooms on the first floor after my speed dial seemingly goes unanswered, I notice a crucial figure of a trifling size to mine standing firmly in the dark, and the figure grows closer and closer.

"How's your cup of tea?"

The second she finishes her rhetorical question, I've realised that the girl playing hero planning to save one of the preys from the huntsman ended up dying from accidentally stepping on the poisonous ground. She unknowingly turns into the prey. As for the rest of the flocks, their integrity is still unknown.

I am now facing the hunter.

A demon, in the body of a child; that's how I see it, because the yellow eyes I'm seeing right now are no human's. That or I'm just hallucinating.

The girl mumbles loudly a train of words that I can't be... all ears. I can hear them alright but I haven't got enough breath to listen, and there are so many words passing through my trembling station without me being able to get on board in any one of them. I don't know how long she has been speaking as my hopeless body starts to depart besides the bathtub. But just when it looks like she's about to finish her detailed diegesis, Miss Decima suddenly barges in the door. Thank God!

Or so I thought.

Idonia's lips are sealed speechless at the view that Miss Decima is still alive. She's never made aware of the news of her expected burial, not even her flourishing escape from death. As the broadcasting company was never permitted to declare the news, Idonia forced herself to the belief of a presumably coma going on.

As Miss Decima slowly strolls nearer, there's a shiny but blurry object lifted up by her right hand. It's a black crystal, then blinks into a dagger, then a rope, then a gun, and then back to a dagger.

I can now see her face clearer as she comes closer. She first looks angelic worried but then smiles in a demon way that much resembles my first impression of her. Just coincidentally too, a man all of a sudden breaks in behind Miss Decima, much to her surprise.

It's Detective Jevon who comes to my rescue; but perhaps he is not, as his face also changes from the face of a familiar hero that I'm desperately in need into a villain of when a foreign enemy desires my death.

Right at this very moment, I'm forced to close my eyes as my willingness to live can no longer hold my body shutting down. I can no longer regret myself, I can no longer blame my life.

I'm dead.

42

~

The Truth

The moribund of my departure takes me backward like a jet coaster to the first moment it all started, as perhaps the Creator deems me worthy to hover on the truth - the whole truth - upon my endeavour.

The set of events is cascading like swirling red wine inside a crystal glass while I'm drowning slowly, but everyone is not all at the same time in it. The story is flowing like truth, moving like reverie.

All fires and bullets are coming out of Gershom Pavirsia and Petunia Eastaughffe like a war. The woman has been found cheating, the man snooping with full suspicion and finding out more than he expected. Instead of keeping their horrible secret irrelevant, they're speaking too much by deeming them relevant, thus blurted out unintentionally all the horrible things they had done to Idonia. They don't know that the little girl is just on the other side of the door, listening. Tormented by those blooded words, she runs away into the nearest hiding place she can find, a little opening where air passes in and out in secret; her innocent mind surrenders inside and turns dark as she pushes her palms hard against her ears.

For keeping her beauty and image is priority, Petunia switches the lever from a monster in anger to a complete saint. She proceeds with the party she throws in regularly with the blooded fortunes she's shortly blessed with, in which Gershom defeatedly gives in; but he unconsciously releases his bolted anger by loving the child he used to think of his, less and less, then no more.

Decima Somerset, escaping the scandalous non-productive conversations that are boring her to death, walks out of the garden unannounced while leaving her silver clutch behind. Wilbert Cruikshank sees the answer to his problems to fund his remote interest, encouraging himself to waste no time in snatching it. With the powerful little card on his hand, he's able to purchase the black crystal and start his newest experiment in no time. Little does he realise, Idonia sees what he does from the balcony above.

Wilbert confesses his fault; but to his surprise, Idonia promises not to tell anyone if his experiment shows to be amusing. The old man conveys his uncontrollable wicked desire by grating the great crystalline in front of the two live audience not suitable for the view. The black dust retrieved from its source is then forcefully breathed in by the little mouse from the garden, a creature the old man severely hates for eating the crops; and after it demonstrates its misery from the poisonous side effects of the rock, its life comes to an end. Tamerlane Cruikshank leaves the place horrified by the presentation, but not Idonia who draws fascination by it and eventually brings the show to her sleep then writes the evil plan in her dream.

Then the action begins.

She witnesses what a small dose does to a little being, but what she wants to know next is how much it does to a human being. As such, she steals back the crystal at night and shaves it at her new hiding spot, the vent. She knows she needs to be careful, as at the first go she could expose the poison back to herself instead; she is exceedingly smarter than the average. To cover her tracks, she moves through the vent releasing the ghostly sound the rest of the house grasps in, then gets back to her room. While everyone is scared inside their blankets with their own imaginations, she travels by foot downstairs and then puts the dust from inside her pendant and tests it on the sleeping Wilbert right under his nose for this is now his turn to inhale; and so when he dies in the morning, no one will ever find out of the missing crystal or the existence. The dose she increases from the measurement of a twenty centimetre size of a mouse to a five feet and seven tall man, as it turns out, has turned to be an overdose, as the man immediately gives in to his unforeseen agony and eventually breathes out his one last breath. And what does she feel witnessing all of this?

"So this is what it feels like, Mamma," she mutters as a printed old article crumples on the side yielded from her grip.

Nothing else, in particular, she finds of novelty. She needs a new toy.

She tests her patience this time, and it is by slowly putting pinch by pinch of it in the cup of tea of her other 'mommy' in the next three months to further curse her for being utterly blindsided by the gold rush. The soaring tower falls unknowingly and hopelessly slowly as the termite has managed to devour her vigorous establishment brick by brick. The night before the birth tribute, the little girl, after being able to analyse the habit of the cup in and out, sneaks into the kitchen with the same scare systematically, and manages to seed not one but two glasses of wine altogether for a purpose, known achievement as their punishment. She thinks the second dose of poison will get the medical officer his own demise for the betrayal he surrenders into. Well little girl, some of the grimes are just not ready to come out enough, and the darkness in the room that is no more sunless than your heart has justified one's o'clock on this earth should have been more for you to value, as you close the sundial too soon, and the doctor is aware of his apparatus hygiene too much.

She has successfully made the doctor miserable in another way, unintentionally, but the one out of two is not the way it is supposed to be done; she thinks as she admits to the sky, "Mamma, I have failed."

The poor widower who in a matter of one night turns to remorse for his evermore love that is gone. Someone he loved is about to kill him the same way the *emerald spherule* mechanism works. Right the night before the burial, the little girl scares the whole house to their bed and goes into the room of someone she loved and puts the poison from her pendant in his morning water, steals the key to the study room for the dagger while unconsciously smears the dust onto the weapon, and puts the key back where it belongs.

That is not enough, she thinks, for the person who doesn't love her anymore for who or *what* she is deserves the dagger to free fall from the sky as punishment, as she has bestowed when she goes through the vent and does exactly as it is; with the lengthen skill she has had for the ball, so does the dagger with no remorse. The last thing he is forced to see before his death is the child he has not been able to glimpse with his courage any more. What a coincidence that the lamb is going into the abattoir, just the exact moment he turns his back from the other lamb who then was slayed.

"Mamma, we are almost the same," the killer whispers.

In a flash, her mother comes to visit her in her dream; or maybe herself disguised as her mother.

"Idonia," she says, "we are never different, and therefore I will never leave you."

"Yes, Mamma, and for that, I will finish what I have started, the same way you did."

She prints the printed article of her mother's accomplishments and what better to be done than burning the paper to the ground, hoping to lift the spirit alive, and amalgamates the mass to the substance living inside the hourglass on her neck.

"Come, Mamma," as she reenacts the groundless ritual she once saw on television without anyone noticing, or even caring how she can get that match that can burn her.

The same way she scares humankind, only this time she does not choose to stay inside; she is out in the open. Much alive and ready for more.

After she breaks in through the vent, the only passage she perfectly knows how, she forces the poisonous dust to be breathed in by the hopeless widow. She blames the gossip her butlers and maids share between themselves, for that's the only way she knows about the old lady's depression. Between the certitude that Edda Burwood is no longer willing to live and the perseverance the petite old woman wrestles the alien necklace that she is not ready to give in, the young girl wraps the match by dragging the stranger's lifeless body and does what she plans with the new tie knot skill no one knows she can. She thinks her 'mamma' gives her additional strength.

"Mamma, now, we are exactly the same," she speaks in consolation.

As much as she feels all of her biologicals that she's from are gone, and as much as she is aware that her true father is still alive, she will not take abandonment as an excuse for letting him alive. And as none as Halihan Dunbar knows, the young girl has successfully infiltrated the pyramid of gold belonging to her and buries himself along with it inside, as he chokes and drowns to death beneath his presents of glory.

"Mamma, this is for you," she declares before she leaves.

How does the traces from inside of the little girl's time-sand ever come in contact with one of Decima Somerset's cigarettes, and at such short notice too? It all lies in the word 'Cigarette'. The mysterious figure with a cloak on her head is hiding herself carefully while writing the word on the little note unconsciously so beautifully due to her day job as a respectable homeschool teacher. Miss Gretchen Danburry has the habit of teaching her students how to write so perfectly.

She at length feels there's no choice as the young girl, as the wicked desperately wants the poisonous cigarette to land on Decima at the perfect time in which she has been failing to plan so, blackmails the educator in her greatest weakness before death herself, to bring her to the art gallery as she sneaks in the cigarette while Decima leaves her bag on the bench to analyse the waves few steps closer further. How fate weeps that Daedalia goes in the entrance of the gallery right a few seconds after they leave the building and never catches her face in due. For this sin she has regretfully been a part of, she leaves the job that pays her more than commonly; but the leaving saves her life as she is due to be killed someday somewhere if Idonia still sees her around. The secret is safe with her as she is to never land another job if the little girl is found to be evil under her care.

"Good job, Miss Gretchen," Idonia grins to her sinful achievement whereas the governess cries of mortal mind agony as she realises she takes part in the attempted murder.

As for Oriel Walmsley, poor greedy Oriel, it seems that she never even has the chance in the first place as soon as she breaks in into Godric Simpkin's house in her own accord, as the little girl too has been waiting for her alongside the air in the confined space just her size. Instead of expecting the legal document of Bailhache's fortunes as provoked by Idonia, she instead counters a bullet raging into her frame.

"One for the money and two for the dummy," as she fires the gun perfectly close to the ageing woman, to ensure accuracy.

Getting the gun is no mystery, not as much as the fact that she has been hiding one after Gershom's death, right inside her green magical ball that can do anything. The magic does not stop there, as Godric is seen carrying Oriel's body. This is due to his overconsumption of the sleeping pill. The sleeping pill makes him unconsciously dispose of the body after hearing the gunshots, perfectly sleeping while still naturally awake doing it.

Nonetheless, the little girl does not expect that one, just one of the cameras actually catches one tenth portion of her dress that night, and two third of her face, if the police had not been so invested in the wrongfully accused aftermath. Just like when Daedalia didn't expect the arsenic shave she put in her cup of tea that Durcel had brought for her that night, with her successful attempt on distracting her with the broken plate in the kitchen.

"It is complete, Mamma," that is all that matters to her.

All the red wine has now been spilled out of the cordial glass.

I guess the next real question is this. Am I still dead?

43

❧

Heaven

I wake up to a fresh smell of lavender, swaying happily to the oppression of the breeze that adequately carries the scent to my senses. I start to wonder if this is what *heaven* smells like.

As much as I can feel the rigidness blasted upon my body from seemingly half-asleep alone between the truth and the death in this hospital bed for days, I am not dead. I am alive. And, I am not alone.

The doctor said I was dead for longer than about thirty minutes. My body was shut down, but by some miracle I was resuscitated.

"A cardiopulmonary resuscitation performed correctly right on time, and a fine post-resuscitation care afterward," he describes the form of the miracle.

Surprisingly, my parents and my big brother, Damarion, are

circling around me with a big relief shoutout from each one of them. Apparently, I had been unconscious for two days. Then I imagine a day if I were to reach a very old age and I was completely alone; maybe this time I do see a point in getting married and having children.

"This is why you should never play detective *alone*, little sis," my big brother warns me with amused giggles; he wouldn't be laughing if I was dead.

"OR EVER!" My dad suddenly shouts, the loudest he's ever been to any of us; I didn't even know he could scream that loud.

My shoulders jump unexpectedly, as well as the others' around me, and it's only natural that his thunder eventually puts everyone in the room to silence.

Yes, everyone, including Miss Decima whose tears I can see just a bit in her eyes.

I'm hearing everyone, sharing their own version of the story. I laugh when my mother, even though she wasn't even there when I was dying, exaggerates almost the whole story to any of my visitors - those who visit me in person and those virtually. My mom is completely taking over my storytelling duty.

As it appears too, Miss Decima was able to record Idonia's confession in the bathroom while forcing her tears and mucus not to burst after cleverly and quickly calling the ambulance. She immediately barged in the door once Idonia was done. What she didn't see further coming was how Detective Jevon suddenly came to Mrs. Lesley's house too, that she almost thought he was part of the evils when he wasn't; and for that, I have to explain my part.

"I was just following someone's advice to be more careful at a 'poisonous' time like this, and so I called the police station. Apparently, they sent Detective Jevon in," I speak my reason almost with the exact same words she once spoke to me; she smiles proudly, surprised that I still remember.

I didn't really trust Miss Decima; but now, I really do.

What are the chances that you and your best buddy were on the verge of death with the same poison by the same killer? I don't know anything about soulmates, but if there's a list of definite criterias for it, I bet that this will fall into such category.

Coincidentally, I didn't really trust Detective Jevon too, until now. But what I didn't know, when the station mentioned my name, he just happened to be there. He somehow trusted me; and without further ado, he proceeded to the calling without further question.

I guess you can call that the best outcome from trust and luck combined.

Turns out, the coincidences he has been meddling with, they really are coincidences after all. I guess I've just been second guessing and overthinking all the serendipities that happen to surround me since the first murder, covering them with my lack of trust and confidence, and as such I made them the worst. But maybe second guessing and too much thinking sometimes can be good, if only I also second guessed the tea.

At least we all know now who's the real monster.

And she's not a ghost, she just acts like one. At least, that's what I think so far.

Then a few weeks later comes that feels like many years long.

The court has never been this full, I hear from many.

I also see Doctor Godric among the audience. I mean, why not see in person the little girl that was able to almost get you executed? And maybe get her executed in return; I'd reckon this is what his anger sounds like.

Even Bou's attempt to apply for a *research visit* here to attend the trial that she expected to be a 'no' go, turns from 'Submitted' into a surprisingly but happily 'Granted'.

"I would guess the small gap that will differentiate this *evil* little girl's destiny between shelter and execution is this; if she is by nature or nurture, 'evil'," she points out her argument if she was to stand.

As for me, I would guess that my turn to speak is coming very soon.

"Miss Daedalia Pavirsia-Abernathy" to the stand.

44

~

The Trial

As my name is being called by the prosecutor who is deemed by herself and others of no empathy, regardless of her own motherhood, for charging the little girl a first and third degree murder, I'm sworn by the bible to only speak of the truth and nothing but the truth, in front of the little Miss Evil that currently doesn't dare to look at me in the eye. She seems to be... in deep remorse? I'm not too sure.

"Is this the *emerald green spherule*, as the witness calls it, that you took the day you were poisoned?"

I nod to the prosecutor's question.

"Where did you *hide* this on that day?"

"In the trunk of my car," I answer.

Besides, I also promise myself to speak of the truth and nothing but the truth.

"This small crystalline metalloid rock, or may I say *leftovers*, that when shaved with this small grate right here, will form the poisonous arsenic dusts. They are the exact match to the toxic report of every six deceased victims as well as the three attempted murders," Mrs. Ruth Applegate, the prosecutor, lifts the picture of the rock and shows the video of the demonstration to the judge and the jury as well as the rest of the audience.

"And this bell," she goes on, "This is the one removed from the table in the study room where Gershom Pavirsia was killed, by the very same person who detached it before the murder."

"And the rope, ahem, oh, sorry," that is my brain speaking while I once again unconsciously vocalise it, somehow.

Everyone's now looking at me and it's kind of awkward. Maybe I need another rest, not just recovering from the poison, but from the awkward state of affairs I've just created.

Immediately after that, Mrs. Ruth quickly takes over the situation by proceeding on her statement.

"And yes, the rope," as she insinuates on the last part while smiling at me so I feel better about myself.

"The rope, with the exact colour and material that was used to kill Edda Burwood. The end line of this rope, as it was compared to the one used to hang its victim, is a perfect match. That rope is indeed being cut from this rope!" And I think some people almost give her an applause.

"On top of that, this rope, as further analysed by the CSIs which will also take the stand later to corroborate this, you see, when a portion of this was burnt–"

"Objection!" The defence attorney, Mr. Leslie Spector, tries to gain his moment.

"Where is the prosecutor going on with this, Your Honour?" He continues.

"I am getting there, Your Honour, I promise," Mrs. Ruth prattles with the judge, Sir Lemon Pitt (such a cute name), but I think he will be in her favour as the old man seems curious too as to what happened with the rope.

"Overruled! Please proceed, Mrs. Applegate."

And the audience cheers in silence, or maybe it's just me that's cheering.

"When a portion of this rope is burnt, it will create a smell, you see, a distinct smell coming from the defendant's own bedroom. A smell of amber, as this rope from the victim's neck also revealed the exact same scent when burnt. This proves that these ropes came from the same source, Miss Idonia Pavirsia's bedroom."

Afterward, the audience's chatters soon fill up the room, and Sir Lemon has to scream "Silence!" before everyone remembers again where they are, in a courtroom.

"And where was all of this evidence found? This green sophisticated ball right here, all with Idonia Pavirsia's fingerprints all over it, in the witness' car, as she tried to frame her," Mrs. Ruth looks satisfied saying it.

For a second there, I almost think that if I wasn't poisoned, or if I didn't almost die, I may have been... Nevermind. Fortunately, the law and fate sided with me then.

The trial goes on for so many days as the thirteen year-old

female is charged with six murders and three attempted ones, including Doctor Godric's, which is probably why he looks much happier than he usually is. It is, very much so, a peculiar case that attracts many as well as divides in a fair split of support between asylum jail and death penalty for the little girl.

More and more evidence is presented in the trial, and more people come to the stand too as witnesses such as Miss Decima, Miss Gretchen, Mr. Catullus, Adelle, Detective Jevon, countable smart CSIs and field experts, and many others.

"Is this young loveable girl naturally too foul and wicked for the world, or is it the other way around? However, why does the brain structure as scientifically compared between two people, one is perceived as an angel and the other is considered a devil for instance, can be the exact same match with totally different behavioural response to the world? Same as to why one can thrive to control the emotion of a pain and the other does not have any at all. The thing is, as this is the first case that a young adult as such managed to accomplish such heinous crimes and unsympathetic murders to her beloved ones around her, anyone in this country, even the world probably ever witnesses, we will be able to ensure such as last if we treat the young defendant as an adult who has been known all along that what she did was and is forever wrong," Mrs. Ruth Applegate ends her statement by bowing to the jury.

"Idonia's deranged behaviour started when she found out she was not Gershom Pavirsia and Petunia Eastaughffe's biological daughter, which Petunia had known all along with her profit-able scheme completely unknown by Idonia as the main subject to the plan, and as supported by the victim that was bound not to be pregnant. This led to Gershom ignoring the little girl as she was beloved by the man no more. Idonia then started to feel everyone knew; and as she was never cared for, that is what drives her *mad*. You see, this child is just an innocent girl falling into an unconscious victim from her destructive surroundings, nurturing her to kill for blood as her only way that she could think of to cope and survive without the help from anyone," Mr. Leslie Spector therefore concludes the innumerable and very long trial.

45

~

Nurtured Blood

It took the jury about eight months of deliberation, one of the longest ever to be carried out in this country, as no one could ever imagine such a child was capable of doing such horrendous things.

The day the decision is finally put in place.

The jury has reached a verdict. Though the verdict is obvious, it is more of where she goes after the verdict that still really draws blank for many, including me.

"State of Victoria versus Idonia Pavirsia. Case number two zero one seven one two three I P as to the charge of first degree murder. We the jury find as follows as to the defendant in this case, that the defendant is guilty of first degree murder as charged.

The defendant, however, will be transferred to the asylum as immediate as today for six months until she turns fourteen before being transferred to prison for the rest of her life, with no probability for parole."

I can hear many sighs from the audience, but the face of Miss Decima sitting beside me clearly shows that she's unhappy with the result.

"That girl is pure evil, there's no need to keep her alive," Miss Decima says without remorse.

"Hush! Someone can hear you! Don't you think that's too harsh?" I give my response.

Afterward, all of us scatter to leave the place with our own thoughts.

So, is evil by nature or nurtured? No one seems to ever get the answer for that.

At least it's all over now.

Or so we thought.

Almost the exact same day from many years before, when it all started.

Call it a coincidence if you want.

<u>Scroll down for the most recent news</u>
Victoria TV Tube
Time Capsule D|0Y0M|

BREAKING NEWS HEADLINE

(13/12 4:05 PM) BABY OF VICTORIA KILLER FROM 13 YEARS AGO SHOCKINGLY REVEALED TO BE THE SERIAL KILLER |View|

(14/12 11:59 PM) IDONIA THE 13 YEAR-OLD WILLOWDALE KILLER IS DEAD, ALONG WITH FOURTEEN OTHERS |View|

(15/12 7:13 PM) READERS NOTICE COLD-CREEP SIMILARITIES BETWEEN MOTHER-DAUGHTER VICTORIA AND WILLOWDALE KILLER, INCLUDING TIMELINE. WHAT IS GOING ON? |View|

(15/12 11:11 AM) EVIL INTENTION AND CRIMINAL BEHAVIOUR, BY NATURE OR NURTURED? |View|

There is no knowing what is going on in that little head of hers. As it turns out, she managed to sneak in a bit of the rock, a salt-rock size. She grated them onto the wall then she killed as many as fourteen in the asylum; ten residences, three nurses, and one doctor, as well as injured nine others; not just with the arsenic, but pens and any pointed devices she could find. It's said that she went bizarre, before saving the biggest of the smallest *crystalline metalloid* for her own to swallow.

And the rest, the rest is history.

How was she even able to do that? Is there another person we're missing? Or, was it just her destiny?

No one is sure. No one might ever find out too; for instance, whether I gave that piece of rock to her the last time I saw her, to cover my tracks, just in case I was the real mastermind.

Of course, I didn't. Of course, I wasn't.

This evil thought; sometimes I wonder if I have a little bit of that in me too, and I hate it when it plays tricks on me in my head like this. But maybe this world is just full of dark wickedness covered with snow; so long as you're still breathing on this earth, you just can't avoid it. You can still deny it, but you can't really avoid it.

Maybe some people were naturally born angels and some others devils; which one am I? But maybe we're equally both and our surroundings nurture us to be either one of the two. That is just the price we pay to live in this world. There is no end to the debate; and there is simply no right answer to the wrong kind of question, or the other way around.

Born-devil or an angel turned devil, they all end up the same - in hell.

But where is hell anyway?

Killers devouring blood by nature or they're being nurtured to be a monster.

Maybe they both exist and are just living side by side.

But what about Idonia? Maybe the *monster* was unleashed in her when she was without love. I think if she had been loved, she would have stayed the same - an innocent girl who just wants to be loved as much as any little kids and grown ups ever want. She was alone and without love, her past showed her the way for revenge, her surroundings *nurtured* her to kill, her thoughts thirsted her for *blood*.

Why am I even thinking about all this?

I've noticed some recent changes in me actually; this feeling that maybe I'm smarter than stupid, I'm better than inferior; that maybe, I deserve something better for myself than I thought I did. I still don't know what I'm going to be or where I'm going, but I don't think I'm completely lost or that I'm completely useless anymore. For the first time in my life, I think I can really contribute something to the world, any world around me. Maybe because I almost died; technically, I was dead.

So now, I can really go anywhere I want, do anything I want, and I don't even want to care anymore if I'm good enough or not. I'm just going to do it; because I was dead. Am I right?

I'm still lost, there's no denying there. But at least I think I really know where to start this time, and when. And it starts right now.

Not The End

By Priscila K.

The World with No Evil

Nurtured Blood

About the Author

Goes by the name of **Priscila K.**
I don't mean to hide, I'm just fitfully shy;
except when I'm singing and there's no one around me.

An avid writer by heart, a brain truster à la carte.
My thoughts confuse me at times;
I write just to make some sense of myself.

Passionate about the art of storytelling.
I write to vent, I vent to write.

Constantly yearning for a sense of meaning in doing.
I think living without a purpose is the saddest thing in life.

Curious and continuous learning mindset.
I'm a lucid dreamer by nature; what's more, my dreams while I'm
asleep are constantly drawing me into raising a lot of questions.

Presence can often be found in bookstores.
The greatest thing about books;
we can live our deepest fantasies even when we're awake,
just by flipping through the pages - imagination counts as real.
They can even inspire us to be better in life.

Consequently, I can't stop writing.

PriscilaK.com